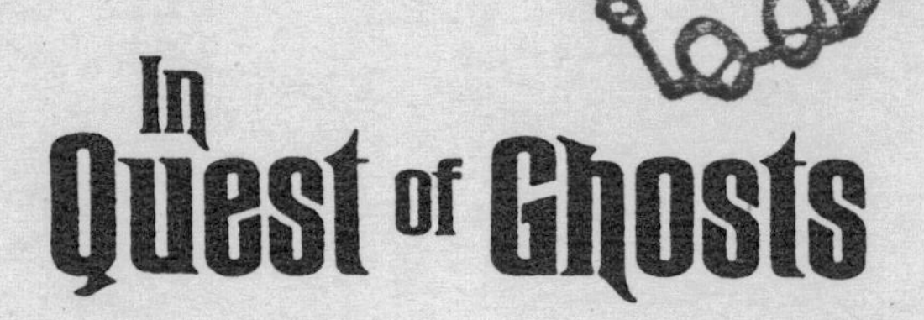


2.00

# In Quest of Ghosts

Hans Holzer

SCHOLASTIC INC.
New York Toronto London Auckland Sydney

Some of the stories in *In Quest of Ghosts* have been published before in slightly different form.



ISBN 0-590-47346-8



12 11 10 9 8 7 6 5 4 3 2 1 3 4 5 6 7 8/9

Printed in the U.S.A. 01

First Scholastic printing, September 1993

# Contents

# In Quest of Ghosts

# Introduction

My interest in ghosts and what most people call "the supernatural" (even though I consider it perfectly natural) started at an early age indeed.

In kindergarten, to be exact.

"Enough of this nonsense," the kindergarten teacher, Miss Seidler, said sternly, and a hush fell upon the assembled children. There were seven or eight boys and girls, roughly four years old, grouped around a boy who sat on a wooden chair in the middle of an imperfect circle. Imperfect was right. The teacher did not approve of our activities. I was the little boy in the middle, and I had been telling the kids some of the wildest ghost stories ever heard anywhere since Edgar Allan Poe was in knee pants.

Tales of the supernatural seemed to come to me easily, as if I had been born to tell them; where I got my raw materials is still a mystery to me. But apparently the plots hit home; parents started to complain that their offspring wouldn't sleep nights, demanding more and better ghost stories; and what the heck were they teaching their youngsters at Miss Seidler's?

It was clear that Miss Seidler did not intend to make ghost-story-telling a regular — or even an irregular — part of the curriculum.

"Hans," she now demanded, "let me see that."

"That" was the book of wisdom I had been holding in my hands, pretending to read from. It was a little futuristic, for I could neither read nor write at that point, but I had seen grown-ups doing it, so I copied the action. My book was no ordinary book, however. It was my father's trolley car pass, expired, in a nice black leather cover. Miss Seidler was not impressed.

After a moment of silence, she returned the pass to me, and told me to stop telling ghost stories.

But you can't keep a good man down. By the time I was six, I was regaling my mother's family in Moravia with tales told me, allegedly, by the wood sprites in the trees along the little river that flows through the city of Bruenn, where I spent every summer. My beginnings in the psychic field were humble, to say the least, and about as far from fact as you can go.

Fortunately, my uncle Henry was a dreamer and understanding. At his side, I had my first whiff of the real thing: Psychic experiences really existed, I was informed, and my interest was now doubly aroused. Uncle Henry, of course, did not treat me like a parapsychologist: I was a boy of maybe nine or ten who liked adventure, and that was precisely what he was going to give me. In his room, furnished exclusively with eighteenth-century furniture and antiques, we held séances by candlelight. He had some early books dealing with unexplained occurences, and used to read from them in distorted Latin. The sound but not the meaning penetrated my consciousness, and it was all very exciting.

Uncle Henry did not say there were ghosts and spirits; neither did he say there weren't. It was all I needed in getting my secret work cut out for me; a responsible adult approved, so I was doing the right thing!

As the years passed, my interests veered toward science and the unconquered territories of electronics and radio. A new rationalism grew in my mind and I became very cocky in my attitude toward anything I could not touch, see, hear, or feel at this point: How *could* such things as spirits exist?

There had to be a "natural" explanation, regardless of the evidence presented! I was completely unwilling to regard an unseen world around us as anything but pure fantasy, as remnants of childhood memories totally incompatible with my brave new world of electronics.

I was about ten at the time, and such silly attitudes were perhaps normal. But I know some mature, intelligent adults who have exactly the same sort of reasoning. There is that television producer, for instance, who patiently listened to all the evidence for the existence of psychic phenomena, looked carefully at the photographs taken under test conditions, and even managed to have an experience with strange pictures himself — to no avail.

"There's got to be some other explanation," he would intone regularly. He, like many others in our materialistic world today, is incapable of accepting the truth unless that truth conforms to his preconceived notions as to what that truth must look like. It is a little like the bed of Procrustes. Procrustes, you may recall, was a highwayman in ancient Greece whose particular brand of fun consisted of placing unwary travelers into his "special" bed: If they were too long, he'd cut them down; if they were too short, he'd stretch them to fit.

I did not attend the ordinary, tuition-free high school in my ancestral city of Vienna, Austria, but managed to get into a *Gymnasium*, a combination of high school and junior college, with emphasis on the humanities. My electronics spirit had somehow departed along the way, and was now replaced by a burning desire to become an archaeologist. Children often change their plans dozens of times during their school days, depending on what influences them in the world around them. But in my case, at least, the label stuck, and I did indeed become an archaeologist — at least at first.

That was in the 1930s, when Europe seethed with political unrest and the madman of Berlin had already cast a heavy shadow upon smaller countries around Germany, such as the Austria I grew up in. It seemed foolish, on the face of it, to study history and the humanities in *Gymnasium* in order to continue at the university in the hopes of becoming an archaeologist, at a time when more practical pursuits might have been wiser. I also evinced a strong interest in writing, and it was clear to me that I would be a *Schriftsteller*, an author, of some kind — exactly what I have become. But in the 1930s, when I was in my early teens, this was really quite outlandish to my parents and friends.

In the second half of my *Gymnasium* period, when I was sixteen years old, I was profoundly impressed by one of my teachers, Franz Spunda. This brought me into immediate disrepute with most of my classmates, since he was one of the least-liked teachers and one of the most feared.

The reasons for this were in the man's character: He was a taciturn, dour man who seldom joked or said an unnecessary word, and whose scholastic behavior was stern and uncompromising. Other teachers you could soften up, but not him. What impressed me about Franz Spunda, however, was not the fact that he was disliked by my classmates, of course, for I am not a nonconformist for its own sake. Spunda was a well-known writer of historical novels who, like so many authors, even successful ones, was forced to augment his income by teaching.

Perhaps he resented this, for it interfered with his more important work, but his storehouse of knowledge was greater than called for in his teaching position. His classes dealt with literature, as was to be expected, but I soon discovered that Dr. Spunda had a deep interest in parapsychology, just as I used to have in the old Uncle Henry days.

I read some of Spunda's books, which led to the

very technical books on parapsychology by Professor Oesterreicher and by G. W. Gessmann, both published in the 1920s, which I acquired in 1935 when I was fifteen. Suddenly I realized that there was truth in these accounts, and that it was worthy of my further efforts to involve myself in the study of the occult. Whenever I had an opportunity, I let Dr. Spunda know that I shared his interests in these fields. On one occasion, I picked as the topic for a paper the rather cumbersome title of "Dr. von Schrenck-Notzing's Theory of the Telekinetic, Teleplastic, Ideolplasticity," and confounded my classmates just by the title, to say nothing of the contents!

But not Dr. Spunda. After I was through, he remarked that it was a hodgepodge of several theories and proceeded to criticize my statements with the experienced approach of an inside man. After this, it became clear to my classmates that I was something special, and many avoided me afterward in anything but the most superficial relationships. It suited me fine, for I preferred a few close friends to general and shallow popularity.

At the University of Vienna, my days were occupied with the formal studies of archaeology and history; psychic matters had to wait. In 1938, we decided that the threatening war clouds would soon erupt into rainstorms of blood and destruction, and I went to live in New York where my father had spent many years at the turn of the century as an immigrant. All this time, my interest in the world of the sixth sense lay dormant, though far from dead. In 1946, I met for the first time Eileen Garrett, whose work has influenced my thinking profoundly, even though we do not always agree on the conclusions to be drawn from it.

Mrs. Garrett was not only one of the world's greatest mediums, she was also the president of the Parapsychology Foundation, which at one time sponsored my research and that of many others in the field, including the famous "father of ESP," Prof. Joseph B. Rhine of Duke University.

At this point in my studies, I was still trying to find some "natural" way of explaining the phenomena I had witnessed, to correlate them with the known facts of science and nature, even though they might be new aspects or little-known facts within the customary framework of human knowledge and understanding. But the Rockland case threw me for a loop: For all intents and purposes, this was not a shallow impression of a past event, but a seemingly living human being from the past, temporarily using the body of the medium to act out his problems.

I could not reconcile what I observed with the concept of a "dead" impression left behind in the atmosphere, devoid of all further life or power to react to those making a fresh contact with it. I began to get uncomfortable as I realized what I was trying to do: Select my evidence not on the basis of truth, but instead make the facts fit the theory. Fortunately I am a very honest fellow. I can't live with half-truths and I don't fool myself about anything when I know, deep within me, that it is wrong.

Consequently, it began to dawn on me that there

were psychic cases involving lifeless "impressions" in the atmosphere, and that there were also cases of authentic hauntings, where a human being was continually reliving his past emotional tragedy.

For me, the search was on for the proof of personal survival, that is to say, scientific evidence that man does survive physical death and continues his existence as a full individual in another dimension.

I realized that ghosts were not exactly ideal cases with which to prove or disprove the nature of that "other side" of the universe. It had become clear to me that all ghosts were either psychotic or at least psychologically disoriented minds, not balanced individuals who had passed on. Obviously, if the survival of a personality was a fact, it would be far more common than hauntings, and the evidence for it should be capable of verification on a much larger scale. More people die "normally" than under tragic conditions, and even among the latter class, those turning up as "ghosts" are again a small portion of the total thus "qualified."

Where was I to turn to find evidence for this so-called spirit world about which the spiritualists had been talking so nicely for so long, without ever convincing me of its reality?

As for so many others raised in the upper middle class, all emotional religions were alien to my way of life. I grew up considering spiritualist mediums as either outright fakes or misguided self-styled prophets at best, and the practice of séances in questionable taste. Should I now reverse myself and seek out some medium and try my hand at a séance?

In 1953, I got to know a group that met regularly at the New York headquarters of the Association for Research and Enlightenment, better known as the Edgar Cayce Foundation. This was a study group, and mediums worked with it to learn more about their own abilities. One such budding medium was Ethel Johnson Meyers, who has since become one of our more famous psychics and one of the people I frequently work with in my investigations. At that time, however, she was just a singing teacher with mediumship who wanted to find out more about herself.

Ethel's controls — spirit personalities operating her psychic channels to regulate the flow of information and to keep out intruders — were her late husband Albert and a Tibetan named Toto Himalaya. I must confess that Toto sounded absolutely phony to me, somewhat like a vaudeville Indian making grunting noises and behaving very much like a synthetic Tibetan, or one manufactured by the unconscious of the medium herself. This, of course, is an age-old question: Are these "controls" real people or are they parts of the personality of the medium that act out consciously during a trance and which the medium cannot act out when awake?

I have never been able to prove satisfactorily the reality of these controls, and some trance mediums like Sybil Leek don't have them. But I haven't any evidence to say that they are anything except what they claim to be, and am of late persuaded to accept them as indeed real human beings who have crossed the threshold into the nonphysical world. Even so great a medium and human being as Eileen Garrett has not been able to make up her own mind on this difficult question.

When I first met Toto via the entranced Ethel Meyers we had our difficulties, for I don't take kindly to generalities and bits of philosophy that waste both a medium's and an investigator's time.

But if Toto was indeed an ancient Tibetan priest, he had a right to preach. I just wasn't particularly ready to listen to the sermon at that point. Instead, I decided to test Ethel's psychometry talents. Psychometry is the gift of touching an object and describing instantly its history or owners. Naturally, the medium must not know anything about the object or see its shape or outline, in order to avoid any conscious clues as to its identity.

Consequently, I took the object I had in mind, wrapped it several times in paper, then in pieces of cloth, until it became a shapeless parcel of about an arm's length and weighing perhaps three pounds. With this thing under my arm, I came down to the Association, where Ethel Meyers was already in the midst of psychometrizing objects. At the first free moment, I thrust the parcel into her outstretched hands and watched for her reactions.

For a moment Mrs. Meyers sat as if stunned. Then, with a shriek, she rose from her chair, at the same time throwing the parcel onto the floor as if I had handed her a stick of dynamite with a lit fuse. Even though it was early spring, she was sweating and I could tell she was upset.

"I see a sacrifice," she mumbled, and shuddered.

"This is some kind of ceremony . . . a dagger . . . don't like it." She looked at me sternly, almost reproachfully.

"It's all right, Ethel," I said, "I shan't ask you to touch it again."

With that, I picked up the package and started to unravel it. The others present had formed a circle around us as layer upon layer of cloth and paper disappeared. Eventually, I held in my hand a gleaming *dorje* or Tibetan sacrificial scepter, at the end of which was a dagger. I had meant to make Toto Himalaya feel at home, and all I had succeeded in doing was getting Mrs. Meyers upset!

The following year, after attending dozens upon dozens of meetings at the Association, I made a special visit because my friends had told me of a new medium who had joined the experimental group and seemed interesting. I was late in arriving and took a seat in the rear of the darkened room. At the far end, a woman sat with her eyes closed, while a small red light burned next to her, casting an eerie glow over the assembled people.

This went on for about fifteen minutes — utter silence while the medium slept. Then she awoke and gave messages to some of those present. It was her brand of mediumship, this going out "alone," and then returning and talking. Most mediums go into trance and talk during, not after, the trance state. The lights came on now, and I arose to leave. I had walked down the corridor when the medium I had just observed came after me and stopped me.

"Are you Hans Holzer?"

I nodded, sure someone had told her my name. But, as I later discovered, nobody had.

"Then I have a message for you. From an uncle."

Now I have lots of uncles, some dead, some living, and I was not impressed. I looked at her blankly.

The dark-haired woman shook her head impatiently.

"His initials are O. S." she said rapidly, "and he's got a wife named Alice. She's a blonde."

All at once I felt shivers down my spine.

Many years before, an uncle of mine named Otto Stransky had died tragically. I was not particularly close to him, and had not thought of him for years. There had been no reason to do so; his family lived thousands of miles away, in South America, and there was almost no contact. Whatever it was, the medium certainly had not read my unconscious mind.

His wife's name was indeed Alice. When he had been alive, she had been a blonde, but by now, however, Alice's hair had long since turned white. Yet, to the timeless memory of her loving husband, the hair would forever be blonde!

That was the first time I had come in contact with a clearcut message from a departed relative or friend that could not be explained by fraud, coincidence, mind reading, or some otherwise explainable cause. It had to be the survival of human personality. I thanked the lady, not realizing at the time that she would also play a large role in my future work. She is probably one of the finest clairvoyant mediums in America today. Her name is Betty Ritter.

Now I knew that in some instances at least, proof of survival could be shown. Then why not in all? Why not, indeed. My mind was made up to turn my attention to this end: to give the average person the facts of afterlife, in terms he or she can both understand and accept; to be a scientist but not a negative doubter. Truth does not need interpretation, just exposure.

That's how I became a Psychic Investigator.

It would be many more years before, on the insistence of the late Eileen Garrett, I would put down in book form the first of my series of real ghost hunts. That book was *Ghost Hunter* — an immediate and resounding success, selling eleven editions and all kinds of foreign adaptations . . . not to mention the fact that it brought me into television, first as a guest with an interesting book and point of view, and eventually, as in the TV series *In Search Of* . . . as on-camera person, writer, and producer. Today, as I write these lines, two national television series are in the works in which I will participate.

Prof. Hans Holzer, Ph.D.

# 1
# Ghosts of the American War of Independence

The struggle for liberty by the American colonists provides some of the most dramatic and fascinating true ghost stories. Names familiar to all of us suddenly become living people.

Nathan Hale, as every schoolchild knows, was the American spy hanged by the British. He was captured at Huntington Beach and taken to Brooklyn for trial. How he was captured is a matter of some concern to the people of Huntington, Long Island. The town was originally settled by colonists from Connecticut who were unhappy with the situation in that colony. There were five principal families who accounted for the early settlement of Huntington, and to this day their descendants are the most prominent families in the area. They were the Sammes, the Downings, the Busches, the Pauldings, and the Cooks. During the Revolutionary War, feelings were about equally divided among the town people: Some were Revolutionaries and some remained Tories. The consensus of historians is that members of these five prominent families, all of whom were Tories, were responsible for the betrayal of Nathan Hale to the British.

All this was brought to my attention by Mrs. Geraldine P. of Huntington. Mrs. P. grew up in what she considers the oldest house in Huntington, although the Huntington Historical Society claims that theirs is even older. Be that as it may, it was there when the Revolutionary War started. Local legend has it that an act of violence took place on the corner of the street, which was then a crossroads in the middle of a rural area. The house in which Mrs. P. grew up stands on that street. Mrs. P. suspects that the capture — or, at any rate, the betrayal — of the Revolutionary agent took place on that crossroads. When she tried to investigate the history of her house, she found little cooperation on the part of the local historical society. It was a conspiracy of silence, according to her, as if some people wanted to cover up a certain situation from the past.

The house had had a "strange depressing effect on all its past residents," according to Mrs. P. Her own father, who studied astrology and white magic for many years, has related an incident that occurred several years ago in the house. He awoke in the middle of the night in the master bedroom because he felt unusually cold. He became aware of "something" rushing about the room in wild, frantic circles. Because of his outlook and training, he spoke up, saying, "Can I help you?" But the rushing about became even more frantic. He then asked what was wrong and what could be done. But no communication was possible. When he saw that he could not communicate with the entity, Mrs. P.'s father finally said, "If I can't help you, then go away." There was a snapping sound, the room suddenly became quiet and warm again, and he went back to sleep. There have been no other recorded incidents at the house in question. But Mrs. P. wonders if some guilty entity wants to manifest, not necessarily Nathan Hale, but perhaps someone connected with his betrayal.

At the corner of 43rd Street and Vanderbilt Avenue, Manhattan, one of the busiest and noisiest spots in all of New York City, there is a small commemorative plaque explaining that Nathan Hale, the Revolutionary spy, was executed on that spot by the British. I doubt that too many New Yorkers are aware of this, or can accurately pinpoint the location of the tragedy. It is even less likely that a foreigner would know about it. When I suggested to my good friend Sybil Leek that she accompany me to a psychically important spot for an experiment, she readily agreed. Despite the noises and the heavy traffic — the spot being across from Grand Central Station — Sybil bravely stood with me on the street corner and tried to get some sort of psychic impression.

"I get the impression of food and drink," Sybil said. I pointed out that there were restaurants all over the area, but Sybil shook her head. "No, I was thinking more of a place for food and drink, and I don't mean in the present. It is more like an inn, a transit place, and it has some connection with the river. A meeting place, perhaps, some sort of inn. Of course, it is very difficult in this noise and with all these new buildings here."

"If we took down these buildings, what would we see?"

"I think we would see a field and water. I have a strong feeling that there is a connection with water and with the inn. There are people coming and going — I sense a woman, but I don't think she's important. I am not sure . . . unless it would mean foreign. I hear a foreign language. Something like *Verchenen.* [Verplanck's Point, on the Hudson River, was a Revolutionary strongpoint at the time.] I can't quite get it. It is not German."

"Is there anything you feel about this spot?"

"This spot, yes. I think I want to go back two hundred years at least; it is not very clear, 1769 or 1796. That is the period. The connection with the water puzzles me."

"Do you feel an event of significance here at any time?"

"Yes. It is not strong enough to come through to me completely, but sufficiently *drastic* to make me feel a little nervous."

"In what way is it drastic?"

"Hurtful, violent. There are several people involved in this violence. Something connected with water, papers connected with water, that is part of the trouble."

Sybil then suggested that we go to the right to

see if the impressions might be stronger at some distance. We went around the corner and I stopped. Was the impression any stronger?

"No, the impression is the same. Papers, violence. For a name, I have the impression of the letters P.T. Peter. It would be helpful to come here in the middle of the night, I think. I wish I could understand the connection with water, here in the middle of the city."

"Did someone die here?"

Sybil closed her eyes and thought it over for a moment. "Yes, but the death of this person was important at that time and indeed necessary. But there is more to it than just the death of the person. The disturbance involves lots of other things, lots of other people. In fact, two distinct races were involved, because I sense a lack of understanding. I think that this was a political thing, and the papers were important."

"Can you get anything further on the nature of this violence you feel here?"

"Just a disturbed feeling, an upheaval, a general disturbance. I am sorry I can't get much else. Perhaps if we came here at night, when things are quieter."

I suggested we get some tea in one of the nearby restaurants. Over tea, we discussed our little experiment, and Sybil suddenly remembered an odd experience she had had when visiting the Biltmore Hotel before. "I receive many invitations to go to this particular area of New York," Sybil explained, "and when I go I always get the feeling of repulsion to the extent where I may be on my way down and get into a telephone booth and call the people involved and say, 'No, I'll meet you somewhere else.' I don't like this particular area we just left; I find it very depressing. I *feel trapped.*"

I am indebted to R. M. Sandwich of Richmond, Virginia, for an intriguing account of an ESP experience he has connected to Patrick Henry. Mr. Sandwich stated that he has had only one ESP experience and that it took place in one of the early estate-homes of Patrick Henry. He admitted that the experience altered his previously dim view of ESP. The present owner of the estate has said that Mr. Sandwich has not been the only one to experience strange things in that house.

The estate-home where the incident took place is called Pine Flash and is presently owned by E. E. Verdon, a personal friend of Mr. Sandwich. It is located in Hanover County, about fifteen miles outside of Richmond. The house was given to Patrick Henry by his father-in-law. After Henry had lived in it for a number of years, it burned to the ground and was not rebuilt until fifteen years later. During that time Henry resided in the old cottage, which is directly behind the house, and stayed there until the main house had been rebuilt. This cottage is frequently referred to in the area as the honeymoon cottage of young Patrick Henry. The new house was rebuilt exactly as it had been before the fire. As for the cottage, which is still in excellent condition, it is thought to be the oldest wood frame dwelling in Virginia. It may have been there even before Patrick Henry lived in it.

On the Fourth of July, 1968, the Sandwiches had been invited to try their luck at fishing in a pond on Mr. Verdon's land. Since they would be arriving quite early in the morning, they were told that the oars to the rowboat, which they were to use at the pond, would be found inside the old cottage. They arrived at Pine Flash sometime around 6 A.M. Mrs. Sandwich started unpacking their fishing gear and food supplies, while Mr. Sandwich decided to inspect the cottage. Although he had been to the place several times before, he had never actually been inside the cottage itself.

Here then is Mr. Sandwich's report.

"I opened the door, walked in, and shut the door tight behind me. Barely a second had passed after I shut the door when a strange feeling sprang over me. It was the kind of feeling you would experience if you were to walk into an extremely cold, damp room. I remember how still everything was, and then I distinctly heard footsteps overhead in the attic. I called out, thinking perhaps there was someone upstairs. No one answered; nothing. At that time I was standing directly in front of an old fireplace. I admit I was scared half to death. The footsteps were louder now and seemed to be coming down the thin staircase toward me. As they passed me, I felt a cold, crisp, odd feeling. I started looking around for something, anything that could have caused all this. It was during this time that I noticed the closed door open very, very slowly. The door stopped when it was half-opened, almost beckoning me to take my leave, which I did at great speed! As I went through that open door, I felt the same cold mass of air I had experienced before. Standing outside, I watched the door slam itself, almost in my face! My wife was still unpacking the car and claims she neither saw nor heard anything."

Revolutionary figures have a way of hanging on to places they liked in life. Candy Bosselmann of Indiana has had a long history of psychic experiences. She is a budding trance medium and not at all ashamed of her talents. In 1964, she happened to be visiting Ashland, the home of Henry Clay, in Lexington, Kentucky. She had never been to Ashland, so she decided to take a look at it. She and other visitors were shown through the house by an older man, a professional guide, and Candy became somewhat restless listening to his historical ramblings. As the group entered the library, and the guide explained about the beautiful ash paneling taken from surrounding trees (for which the home is named), she became even more restless. She knew very well that it was the kind of feeling that forewarned her of some sort of psychic event. As she was looking over toward the fireplace, framed by two candelabra, she suddenly saw a very tall, white-haired man in a long black frock coat standing next to it. One elbow rested on the mantel, and his head was in his hand, as if he were pondering something very important.

Miss Bosselmann was not at all emotionally involved with the house. In fact, the guided tour bored her, and she would have preferred to be outside in the stables, since she has a great interest in horses. Her imagination did not conjure up what she saw: She knew in an instant that she was looking at the spirit imprint of Henry Clay.

In 1969, she visited Ashland again, and this time she went into the library deliberately. With her was a friend who wasn't at all psychic. Again, the same restless feeling came over her. But when she was about to go into trance, she decided to get out of the room in a hurry.

Rock Ford, the home of General Edward Hand, is located four miles south of Lancaster, Pennsylvania, and commands a fine view of the Conestoga River. The house is not a restoration but a well-preserved eighteenth-century mansion, with its original floors, railings, shutters, doors, cupboards, panelings, and window glass. Even the original wall painting can be seen. It is a four-story brick mansion in the Georgian style, with the rooms grouped around a center hall in the design popular during the latter part of the eighteenth century. The rooms are furnished with antiquities of the period, thanks to the discovery of an inventory of General Hand's estate which permitted the local historical society to supply authentic articles of daily usage wherever the originals had disappeared from the house.

Perhaps General Edward Hand is not as well-known as a hero of the American Revolution as others are, but to the people of the Pennsylvania Dutch country he is an important figure, even though he was of Irish origin rather than German. Trained as a medical doctor at Trinity College, Dublin, he came to America in 1767 with the Eighteenth Royal Irish Regiment of Foote. However, he resigned British service in 1774 and came to Lancaster to practice medicine and surgery. With the fierce love of liberty so many of the Irish possess, Dr. Hand joined the Revolutionaries in July of 1775, becoming a lieutenant colonel in the Pennsylvania Rifle Battalion. He served in the army until 1800, when he was discharged as a major general. Dr. Hand was present at the Battle of Trenton, the Battle of Long Island, the Battle of White Plains, the Battle of Princeton, the campaign against the Iroquois, and the surrender of Cornwallis at Yorktown. He also served on the tribunal which convicted Major John Andre, the British spy, and later became the army's adjutant general. He was highly regarded by George Washington, who visited him in his home toward the end of the war. When peace came, Hand became a member of the Continental Congress and served in the Assembly of Pennsylvania as representative of his area. He moved into Rock Ford when it was completed in 1793 and died there in September 1802.

Today, hostesses from a local historical society serve as guides for the tourists who come to Rock Ford in increasing numbers. Visitors are taken about the lower floor and basement and are told of

General Hand's agricultural experiments, his medical studies, and his association with George Washington. But unless you ask specifically, you are not likely to hear about what happened to the house after General Hand died. To begin with, the General's son committed suicide in the house. Before long the family died out, and eventually the house became a museum since no one wanted to live in it for very long. At one time, immigrants were contacted at the docks and offered free housing if they would live in the mansion. None stayed. There was something about the house that was not as it should be, something that made people fear it and leave it just as quickly as they could.

Mrs. Ruth S. lives in upstate New York. In 1967, a friend showed her a brochure concerning Rock Ford, and the house intrigued her. Since she was traveling in that direction, she decided to pay Rock Ford a visit. With her family, she drove up to the house and parked her car in the rear. At that moment she had an eerie feeling that something wasn't right. Mind you, Mrs. S. had not been to the house before, had no knowledge about it, nor any indication that anything unusual had occurred in it. The group of visitors was quite small. In addition to herself and her family, there were two young college boys and one other couple. Even though it was a sunny day, Mrs. S. felt icy cold.

"I felt a presence before we entered the house and before we heard the story from the guide," she explained. "If I were a hostess there, I wouldn't stay there alone for two consecutive minutes." Mrs.

S. had been to many old houses and restorations before but had never felt as she did at Rock Ford.

It is not surprising that George Washington should be the subject of a number of psychic accounts. Probably the best known (and most frequently misinterpreted) story concerns General Washington's vision, which came to him during the encampment at Valley Forge, when the fortunes of war had gone heavily in favor of the British, and the American army, tattered and badly fed, was just about falling to pieces. If there ever was need for divine guidance, it was at Valley Forge. Washington was in the habit of meditating in the woods at times and saying his prayers when he was quite alone. On one of those occasions he returned to his quarters more worried than usual. As he busied himself with his papers, he had the feeling of a presence in the room. Looking up, he saw opposite him a singularly beautiful woman. Since he had given orders not to be disturbed, he couldn't understand how she had gotten into the room. Although he questioned her several times, the visitor would not reply. As he looked at the apparition, for that is what it was, the general became more and more entranced with her, unable to make any move. For a while he thought he was dying, for he imagined that the apparition of such unworldly creatures as he was seeing at that moment must accompany the moment of transition.

Finally, he heard a voice say, "Son of the Republic, look and learn." At the same time, the visitor extended her arm toward the east, and Washington saw what to him appeared like white vapor at some distance. As the vapor dissipated, he saw the various countries of the world and the oceans that separated them. He then noticed a dark, shadowy angel standing between Europe and America, taking water out of the ocean and sprinkling it over America with one hand and over Europe with the other. When he did this, a cloud rose from the countries thus sprinkled, and the cloud then moved westward until it enveloped America. Sharp flashes of lightning became visible at intervals in the cloud. At the same time, Washington thought he heard the anguished cries of the American people underneath the cloud. Next, the strange visitor showed him a vision of what America would look like in the future, and he saw villages and towns springing up from one coast to the other until the entire land was covered by them.

"Son of the Republic, the end of the century cometh; look and learn," the visitor said. Again Washington was shown a dark cloud approaching America, and he saw the American people fighting one another. A bright angel then appeared wearing a crown on which was written the word UNION. This angel bore the American flag, which he placed between the divided nation, saying, "Remember, you are brethren." At that instant, the inhabitants threw away their weapons and became friends again.

Once more the mysterious voice spoke. "Son of the Republic, look and learn." Now the dark angel put a trumpet to his mouth and sounded three distinct blasts. Then he took water from the ocean and sprinkled it on Europe, Asia, and Africa. As he did so, Washington saw black clouds rise from the countries he had sprinkled. Through the black clouds, Washington could see red lights and hordes of armed men, marching by land and sailing by sea to America, and he saw these armies devastate the entire country, burn the villages, towns, and cities, and as he listened to the thundering of the cannon, Washington heard the mysterious voice saying again, "Son of the Republic, look and learn."

Once more the dark angel put the trumpet to his mouth and sounded a long and fearful blast. As he did so, a light as of a thousand suns shone down from above him and pierced the dark cloud which had enveloped America. At the same time, the angel wearing the word UNION on his head descended from the heavens, followed by legions of white spirits. Together with the inhabitants of America, Washington saw them renew the battle and heard the mysterious voice telling him once again, "Son of the Republic, look and learn."

For the last time, the dark angel dipped water from the ocean and sprinkled it on America; the dark cloud rolled back and left the inhabitants of America victorious. But the vision continued. Once again Washington saw villages, towns, and cities spring up, and he heard the bright angel exclaim, "While the stars remain and the heavens send down dew upon the earth, so long shall the Union last." With that, the scene faded, and Washington beheld once again the mysterious visitor before him.

As if she had guessed his question, the apparition then said: "Son of the Republic, what you have seen is thus interpreted: Three great perils will come upon the Republic. The most fearful is the third, during which the whole world united shall not prevail against her. Let every child of the Republic learn to live for his God, his land, and his Union." With that, the vision disappeared, and Washington was left pondering over his experience.

One can interpret this story in many ways, of course. If it really occurred, and there are a number of accounts of it in existence that lead me to believe that there is a basis of fact, then we are dealing with a case of prophecy on the part of General Washington. It is a moot question whether the third peril has already come upon us, in the shape of World War II, or whether it is yet to befall us. The light that is stronger than many suns may have ominous meaning in this age of nuclear warfare.

Washington himself is said to have appeared to Senator Calhoun of South Carolina at the beginning of the War between the States. At that time, the question of secession had not been fully decided, and Calhoun, one of the most powerful politicians in the government, was not sure whether he could support the withdrawal of his state from the Union. The question lay heavily on his mind when he went to bed one hot night in Charleston, South Carolina. During the night, he thought he awoke to see the apparition of General George Washington standing by his bedside. The general wore his presidential attire and seemed surrounded by a bright outline, as if some powerful source of light shone behind him. On the senator's desk lay the declaration of secession, which he had not yet signed. With Calhoun's and South Carolina's support, the Confederacy would be well on its way, having closed ranks. Earnestly, the spirit of George Washington pleaded with Senator Calhoun not to sign the declaration. He warned him against the impending perils coming to America as a divided nation; he asked him to reconsider his decision and to work for the preservation of the Union. But Calhoun insisted that the South had to go its own way. When the spirit of Washington saw that nothing could sway Senator Calhoun, he warned him that the very act of his signature would be a black spot upon the Constitution of the United States. With that, the vision is said to have vanished.

One can easily explain the experience as a dream, coming as it did at a time when Senator Calhoun was particularly upset over the implications of his actions. On the other hand, there is this to consider: Shortly after Calhoun had signed the document taking South Carolina into the Confederacy, a dark spot appeared on his hand, a spot that would not vanish and for which medical authorities had no adequate explanation.

Mrs. Margaret Smith of Orlando, Florida, has had a long history of psychic experiences. She has personally seen the ghostly monks of Beaulieu, England; she has seen the actual lantern of Joe Baldwin, the famous headless ghost of Wilmington, North Carolina; and she takes her "supernatural" experiences in her stride the way other people feel about their musical talents or hobbies. When she was only a young girl, her grandmother took her to visit the von Steuben house in Hackensack, New Jersey. (General F. W. A. von Steuben was a German supporter of the American Revolution who aided General Washington with volunteers who had come over from Europe because of repressions, hoping to find greater freedom in the New World.) The house was old and dusty, the floorboards were creaking, and there was an eerie atmosphere about it. The house had been turned into an historical museum, and there were hostesses to take visitors through.

While her grandmother was chatting with the guide downstairs, the young girl walked up the stairs by herself. In one of the upstairs parlors she saw a man sitting in a chair in the corner. She assumed he was another guide. When she turned around to ask him a question about the room, he was gone. Since she hadn't heard him leave, that seemed rather odd to her, especially as the floorboards would creak with every step. But being young she didn't pay too much attention to this peculiarity. A moment later, however, he reappeared. As soon as she saw him, she asked the question she had on her mind. This time he did not disappear but answered her in a slow, painstaking voice that seemed to come from far away. When he had satisfied her curiosity about the room, he asked her some questions about herself, and finally asked the one which stuck in her mind for many years afterward — "What is General Washington doing now about the British?"

Margaret was taken aback at this question. She was young, but she knew very well that Washington had been dead for many years. Tactfully, she told him this and added that Harry Truman was now president and that the year was 1951. At this information, the man looked stunned and sat down again in the chair. As Margaret watched him in fascinated horror, he faded away.

The following eloquent statement by Harry Hansen goes a long way in describing the relative importance of so temporary a matter as the fate and capture of a British agent during the Revolutionary War.

"Major John Andre's fateful excursion from General Sir Henry Clinton's headquarters at Number 1 Broadway to the gallows on the hill at Tappan took less than a week of the eighteenth century. It seems incredible that this journey should make memorable the roads he followed, the houses he entered, the roadside wells where he stopped to quench his thirst, the words he spoke. But it did."

In the Tarrytowns, up in Westchester County, places associated with Andre are considered prime tourist attractions. More research effort has been expended on the exploration of even the most minute detail of the ill-fated Andre's last voyage than on some far worthier (but less romantic) historical projects elsewhere. A number of good books have been written about the incident, and John Andre has gone into history as a gentlemanly but losing hero of the American Revolutionary War.

To begin with, the American Revolutionary War was more of a civil war than a war between two nations. Independence was by no means desired by all Americans; in fact, the Declaration of Independence had difficulty passing the Continental Congress and did so only after much negotiating behind the scenes and the elimination of a number of passages, such as those relating to the issue of slavery, considered unacceptable by Southerners. When the Declaration of Independence did become the law of the land — at least as far as its advocates were concerned — there were still those who had not supported it originally and who felt themselves put in the peculiar position of being disloyal to their new country or becoming disloyal to the country they felt they ought to be loyal to. Those who preferred continued ties with Great Britain were called Tories, and numbered among them generally were the more influential and wealthier elements in the colonies. There were exceptions, of course, but on the whole the conservatives did not support the cause of the Revolution by any means. Any notion that the country arose *as a man* to fight the terrible British is pure political make-believe. The issues were deep and manifold, but they might have been resolved eventually through negotiations. There is no telling what might have happened if both England and the United Colonies had continued to negotiate for a better relationship. The civil war in Spain was far more a war between two distinct groups than was the American Revolutionary War. In the latter, friends and enemies lived side by side in many areas, the lines were indistinctly drawn, and members of the same family might support one side or the other. The issue was not between Britain, the invading enemy, and America, the attacked; on the contrary, it was between the renunciation of all ties with the motherland and continued adherence to some form of relationship. Thus, it had become a political issue far more than a purely patriotic or national issue. After all, there were people of the same national background on both sides, and nearly everyone had relatives in England.

Under the circumstances, the question of what constituted loyalty was a tricky one. To the British, the colonies were in rebellion and thus disloyal to the king. To the Americans, anyone supporting the British government after the Declaration of Independence was considered disloyal. But the percentage of those who could not support independence was very large all through the war; far more than a few scattered individuals. While some of these Tories continued to support Britain for personal or commercial reasons, others did so out of honest political conviction. To them, helping a British soldier did not constitute high treason but, to the contrary, was their normal duty. Added to this dilemma was the fact that there were numerous cases of individuals crossing the lines on both sides for local business reasons, to remove women and children caught behind the lines, or to parley about military matters, such as the surrender of small detachments incapable of rejoining their regiments or the obtaining of help for wounded soldiers.

In the fall of 1780 the situation had deteriorated to a standstill of sorts, albeit to the detriment of the American forces. The British were in control of the entire South, and they held New York firmly in their grip. The British sloop *Vulture* was anchored in the middle of the Hudson River opposite Croton Point. In this position, it was not too far from that formidable bastion of the American defense system, West Point. Only West Point and its multiple fortifications stood in the way of total defeat for the American forces.

Picture, if you will, the situation in and around New York. The British Army was in full control of the city, that is to say, Manhattan, with the British lines going right through Westchester County. The Americans were entrenched on the New Jersey shore and on both sides of the Hudson River from Westchester County upward. On the American side were first of all, the regular Continental Army, commanded by George Washington, and also various units of local militia. Uniforms for the militia men ran the gamut of paramilitary to civilian, and their training and backgrounds were also extremely spotty. It would have been been difficult at times to distinguish a soldier of the Revolutionary forces from a civilian.

The British didn't call on the citizens of the area they occupied for special services, but it lay in the nature of this peculiar war that many volunteered to help either side. The same situation that existed among the civilian population in the occupied areas also prevailed where the Revolution was successful. Tory families kept on giving support to the British, and when they were found out they were charged with high treason. Nevertheless, they continued right on supplying aid. Moreover, the lines between British and American forces were not always clearly drawn. They shifted from day to day, and if anyone wanted to cross from north of Westchester into New Jersey, for instance, he might very well find himself in the wrong part of the country if he didn't know his way around or if he hadn't checked the latest information. To make matters even more confusing, Sir Henry Clinton was in charge of the British troops in New York City, while Governor Clinton ruled the state of New York, one of the thirteen colonies, from Albany.

In the spring of 1779 Sir Henry Clinton received letters from an unknown correspondent who signed himself only "Gustavus." From the content of these letters, the British commander knew instantly that he was dealing with a high-ranking American officer. Someone on the American side wished to make contact in order to serve the British cause. Clinton turned the matter over to his capable adjutant general, Major John Andre. Andre, whose specialty was what we call intelligence today, replied to the letters, using the pseudonym John Anderson.

Andre had originally been active in the business world but purchased a commission as a second lieutenant in the British Army in 1771. He arrived in America in 1774 and served in the Philadelphia area. Eventually he served in a number of campaigns and by 1777 had been promoted to captain. Among the wealthy Tory families he became friendly with during the British occupation of Philadelphia was the Shippen family. One of the daughters of that family later married General Benedict Arnold.

Andre's first major intelligence job was to make contact with a secret body of Royalists living near Chesapeake Bay. This group of Royalists had agreed to rise against the Americans if military protection were sent to them. Essentially, Andre was a staff officer, not too familiar with field work and therefore apt to get into difficulties once faced with the realities of rugged terrain. As the correspondence continued, both Clinton and Andre suspected that the Loyalist writing the letters was none other than General Benedict Arnold, and eventually Arnold conceded this.

After many false starts, a meeting took place between General Benedict Arnold, the commander of West Point, and Major John Andre on the night of September 21, 1780, at Haverstraw on the Hudson. At the time, Arnold made his headquarters at the house of Colonel Beverley Robinson, which was near West Point.

The trip had been undertaken on Andre's insistence, very much against the wishes of his immediate superior, Sir Henry Clinton. As Andre was leaving,

Clinton reminded him that under no circumstances was he to change his uniform or to take papers with him. It was quite sufficient to exchange views with General Arnold and then to return to the safety of the British lines.

Unfortunately, Andre disobeyed these commands. General Arnold had with him six papers which he persuaded Andre to place between his stockings and his feet. The six papers contained vital information about the fortifications at West Point, sufficient to allow the British to capture the strongpoint with Arnold's help.

"The six papers which Arnold persuaded Andre to place between his stockings and his feet did not contain anything of value that could not have been entrusted to Andre's memory or at most contained in a few lines in cipher that would not have been intelligible to anyone else," states Otto Hufeland in his book *Westchester County During the American Revolution*. But it is thought that Andre still distrusted General Arnold and wanted something in the latter's handwriting that would incriminate him if there was any deception.

It was already morning when the two men parted. General Arnold returned to his headquarters by barge, leaving Andre with Joshua Smith, who was to see to his safe return. Andre's original plan was to get to the sloop *Vulture* and return to New York by that route. But somehow Joshua Smith convinced him that he should go by land. He also persuaded Andre to put on a civilian coat, which he supplied. General Arnold had given them passes to get through the lines, so toward sunset Andre, Smith, and a servant rode down to King's Ferry, crossing the river from Stony Point to Verplanck's Point and on into Westchester County.

Taking various back roads and little-used paths which made the journey much longer, Andre eventually arrived at a spot not far from Philipse Castle. There he ran into three militia men: John Paulding, Isaac Van Wart, and David Williams. They were uneducated men in their early twenties, and far from experienced in such matters as how to question a suspected spy. The three fellows weren't looking for spies, however, but for cattle thieves which were then plaguing the area. They were on the lookout near the Albany Post Road when Van Wart saw Andre pass on his horse. They stopped him, and that is where Andre made his first mistake. Misinterpreting the Hessian coat Paulding wore (he had obtained it four days before when escaping from a New York prison) and thinking that he was among British Loyalists, he immediately identified himself as a British officer and asked them not to detain him. But the three militia men made him dismount and undress, and then the documents were discovered. It has been said that they weren't suspicious of him at all, but that the elegant boots, something very valuable in those days, tempted them, and that they were more interested in Andre's clothing than in what he might have on him. Whatever the motivation, Andre was brought to Colonel Jameson's headquarters at Sand's Mill, which is called Armonk today.

Jameson sent the prisoner to General Arnold, a strange decision which indicates some sort of private motive. The papers, however, he sent directly to General Washington, who was then at Hartford. Only upon the return of his next-in-command, Major Tallmadge, did the real state of affairs come to light. On Tallmadge's insistence, the party escorting Andre to General Arnold was recalled and brought back to Sand's Mills. But a letter telling General Arnold of Andre's capture was permitted to continue on its way to West Point!

Benedict Arnold received the letter the next morning at breakfast. The general rose from the table, announced that he had to go across the river to West Point immediately, and went to his room in great agitation. His wife followed him, and he informed her that he must leave at once, perhaps forever. Then he mounted his horse and dashed down to the riverside. Jumping into his barge, he ordered his men to row him to the *Vulture*, some seventeen miles below. He explained to his men that he came on a flag of truce and promised them an extra ration of rum if they made it particularly quickly. When the barge arrived at the British vessel, he jumped aboard and even tried to force the bargemen to enter the King's service on the threat of making them prisoners. The men refused, and the *Vulture* sailed on to New York City. On arrival, General Clinton freed the bargemen, a most unusual act of gallantry in those days.

Meanwhile Andre was being tried as a spy. Found guilty by a court-martial at Tappan, he was executed by hanging on October 2, 1780. The three militia men who had thus saved the very existence of the new republic were voted special medals by Congress.

The entire area around Tappan and the Tarrytowns is "Andre" country. At Philipse Castle there is a special exhibit of Andre memorabilia in a tiny closet under the stairs. There is a persistent rumor that Andre was trying to escape from his captors. According to Mrs. Cornelia Beekman, who then lived at the van Cortlandt House in Peekskill, there was in her house a suitcase containing an American army uniform and a lot of cash. That suitcase was to be turned over to anyone bringing a written note from Andre. Joshua Hett Smith, who helped Andre escape after his meeting with Arnold, later asked for the suitcase; however, as Smith had nothing in writing, Beekman refused to give it to him. This story came to light only many years after the Revolution, perhaps because Mrs. Beekman feared to be drawn into a treason trial or because she had some feelings of her own in the matter.

Our next stop was to be the van Cortlandt mansion, not more than fifteen minutes away by car. Obviously, Pat Smith was in a good mood this morning. In her little foreign car she preceded us at such a pace that we had great difficulty keeping up with her. It was a sight to behold how this lady eased her way in and out of traffic with an almost serpentine agility that made us wonder how long she could keep it up. Bravely following her, we passed Sleepy

Hollow Cemetery and gave it some thought. No, we were not too much concerned with all the illustrious Dutch Americans buried there, nor with Washington Irving and nearby Sunnyside; we were frankly concerned with ourselves. Would we also wind up at Sleepy Hollow Cemetery, or would we make it to the van Cortlandt mansion in one piece . . . ?

The mansion itself is a handsome two-story building, meticulously restored and furnished with furniture and artworks of the eighteenth century, some of it from the original house. Turned into a tourist attraction by the same foundation that looked after Philipsburg Manor, the house, situated on a bluff, is a perfect example of how to run an outdoor museum. Prior to climbing the hill to the mansion itself, however, we visited the ferryboat house at the foot of the hill. In the eighteenth century and the early part of the nineteenth century, the river came close to the house, and it was possible for the ships bringing goods to the van Cortlandts to come a considerable distance inland to discharge their merchandise. The Ferryboat Inn seemed a natural outgrowth of having a ferry at that spot: The ferry itself crossed an arm of the Hudson River, not very wide, but wide enough not to be forded on foot or by a small boat. Since so much of these buildings had been restored, I wondered whether Ingrid would pick up anything from the past.

The inn turned out to be a charming little house. Downstairs we found what must have been the public room, a kitchen, and another room, with a winding staircase leading to the upper story. Frankly, I expected very little from this but did not want to offend Pat Smith, who had suggested the visit.

"Funny," Ingrid said, "when I walked into the door, I had the feeling that I had to force my way *through a crowd.*"

The curator seemed surprised at this, for she hadn't expected anything from this particular visit, either. "I can't understand this," she said plaintively. "This is one of the friendliest buildings we have."

"Well, I said, "ferryboat inns in the old days weren't exactly like the Hilton."

"I feel a lot of activity here," Ingrid said. "Something happened here, not a hanging, but connected with one."

We went upstairs, where I stopped Ingrid in front of a niche that contained a contemporary print of Andre's execution. As yet we had not discussed Major Andre or his connection with the area, and I doubt very much whether Ingrid realized there was a connection. "As you look at this, do you have any idea who it is?" I asked.

Ingrid, who is very nearsighted, looked at the picture from a distance and said, "I feel that he may have come through this place at one time." And so he might have.

As we walked up the hill to the van Cortlandt mansion, the time being just right for a visit as the tourists would be leaving, I questioned Pat Smith about the mansion.

"My mother used to know the family who owns the house," Pat Smith began. "Among the last decendants of the van Cortlandts were Mrs. Jean Brown and a Mrs. Mason. This was in the late thirties or the forties, when I lived in New Canaan. Apparently there were such manifestations at the house that the two ladies called the Archbishop of New York for help. They complained that a spirit was 'acting up,' that there was the sound of a coach that no one else could see and other inexplicable noises of the usual poltergeist nature."

"What did they do about it?" I asked.

"Despite his reluctance to get involved, the Archbishop did go up to the manor, partly because of the prominence of the family. He put on his full regalia and went through a ritual of exorcism. Whether or not it did any good, I don't know, but a little later a psychic sensitive went through the house also and recorded some of these noises. As far as I know, none of it was ever published, and for all I know, it may still be there — the specter, that is."

We now had arrived at the mansion, and we entered the downstairs portion of the house. Two young ladies dressed in colonial costumes received us and offered us some cornmeal tidbits baked in the colonial manner. We went over the house from bottom to top, from top to bottom, but Ingrid felt absolutely nothing out of the ordinary. True, she felt the vibrations of people having lived in the house, having come and gone, but no tragedy, no deep imprint, and, above all, no presence. Pat Smith seemed a little disappointed. She didn't really *believe* in ghosts as such, but having had some ESP experiences at Sunnyside, she wasn't altogether sure. At that instant she remembered having left her shopping bag at the Ferryboat Inn. The bag contained much literature on the various colonial houses in the area, and she wanted to give it to us. Excusing herself, she dashed madly back down the hill. She was back in no time, a little out of breath, which made me wonder whether she had wanted to make her solo visit to the Ferryboat Inn at dusk just as *brief* as humanly possible.

In a splendid Victorian mansion surmounted by a central tower, the Historical Society of the Tarrytowns functions as an extremely well-organized local museum as well as a research center. Too prudent to display items of general interest that might be found elsewhere in greater quantity and better quality, the Historical Society concentrates on items and information pertaining to the immediate area. It is particularly strong on pamphlets, papers, maps, and other literature of the area from 1786 onward. One of the principal rooms in the society's museum is the so-called Captors' Room. In it are displays of a sizable collection of material dealing with the capture of Major Andre. These include lithographs, engravings, documentary material, letters, and a chair. It is the chair Andre sat in when he was still a free man at the Underhill home, south of Yorktown Heights. Mrs. Adelaide Smith, the curator, was exceptionally helpful to us when we stated the purpose of our visit. Again, as I always do, I prevented Ingrid from hearing my conversation with Mrs. Smith, or with Miss Smith, who had come along now that she had recovered her shopping bag full of literature. As soon as I could get a moment alone with Ingrid, I asked her to touch the chair in question.

"I get just a slight impression," she said, seating herself in the chair, then getting up again. "There may have been a meeting in here of some kind, or he may have been sentenced while near or sitting in this chair. I think there was a meeting in this room to determine what would happen."

But she could not get anything very strong about the chair. Looking at the memorabilia, she then commented, "I feel he was chased for quite a while before he was captured. I do feel that the chair in this room has something to do with his sentence."

"Is the chair authentic?"

"Yes, I think so."

"Now concerning this room, the Captors' Room, do you feel anything special about it?"

"Yes, I think this is where it was decided, and I feel there were a lot of men here, men from town and from the government."

Had Ingrid wanted to manufacture a likely story to please me, she could not have done worse. Everything about the room and the building would have told her that it was of the nineteenth century, and that the impression she had just described seemed out of place, historically speaking. But those were her feelings, and as a good sensitive she felt obliged to say whatever came into her mind or whatever she was impressed with, not to examine it as to whether it fit in with the situation she found herself in. I turned to the curator and asked, "Mrs. Smith, what was this room used for, and how old is the building itself?"

"The building is about one hundred twenty-five years old; our records show it was built between 1848 and 1850 by Captain Jacob Odell, the first mayor of Tarrytown. It was built as one house, and since its erection two families have lived here. First, there were the Odells, and later Mr. and Mrs. Aussie Case. Mrs. Case is eighty-seven now and retired. This house was purchased for the society to become their headquarters. It has been used as our headquarters for over twenty years."

"Was there anything on this spot before this house was built?"

"I don't know."

"Has anyone ever been tried or judged in this room?"

"I don't know."

Realizing that a piece of furniture might bring with itself part of the atmosphere in which it stood when some particularly emotional event took place, I questioned Mrs. Smith about the history of the chair.

"This chair, dated 1725, was presented to us from Yorktown. It was the chair in which Major Andre sat the morning of his capture, when he and Joshua

Smith stopped at the house of Isaac Underhill for breakfast."

The thoughts going through Andre's head that morning, when he was almost sure of a successful mission, must have been fairly happy ones. He had succeeded in obtaining the papers from General Arnold; he had slept reasonably well, been fed a good breakfast, and was now, presumably, on his way to Manhattan and a reunion with his commanding general, Sir Henry Clinton. If Ingrid felt any meetings around that chair, she might be reaching back beyond Andre's short use of the chair, perhaps into the history of the Underhill home itself. Why, then, did she speak of sentence and capture, facts she would know from the well-known historical account of Major Andre's mission? I think that the many documents and memorabilia stored in the comparatively small room might have created a common atmosphere in which bits and snatches of past happenings had been reproduced in some fashion. Perhaps Ingrid was able to tune in on this shallow but nevertheless still extant psychic layer.

Major Andre became a sort of celebrity in his own time. His stature as a British master spy was exaggerated far out of proportion even during the Revolutionary War. This is understandable when one realizes how close the cause of American independence had come to total defeat. If Andre had delivered the documents entrusted to him by General Arnold to the British, West Point could not have been held. With the fall of the complicated fortifications at the point, the entire North would have soon been occupied by the British. Unquestionably, the capture of Major Andre was a turning point in the war, which had then reached a statement, albeit one in favor of the British. They could afford to wait and sit it out while the Continental troops were starving to death, unable to last another winter.

General Arnold's betrayal was by no means a sudden decision; his feelings about the war had changed some time prior to the actual act. The reasons may be seen in his background, his strong Tory leanings, and a certain resentment against the command of the Revolutionary Army. He felt he had not advanced quickly enough; the command at West Point was given him only three months prior to Andre's capture. Rather than being grateful for the belated recognition of his talents by the Continental command, Arnold saw it as a godsend to fulfill his own nefarious task. For several months he had been in correspondence with Sir Henry Clinton in New York, and his decision to betray the cause of independence was made long before he became commander of West Point.

But Andre wasn't the master spy later accounts try to make him out to be: His bumbling response when captured by the three militia men shows that he was far from experienced in such matters. Since he had carried on his person a *laissez-passer* signed by General Arnold, he needed only to produce this document and the men would have let him go. Instead, he *volunteered* the information that he was a British officer. All this because one of the militia men wore a Hessian coat. It never occured to Andre that the coat might have been stolen or picked up on the battlefield! But there was a certain weakness in Andre's character, a certain conceit, and the opportunity of presenting himself as a British officer on important business was too much to pass up when he met the three nondescript militia men. Perhaps his personal vanity played a part in this fateful decision; perhaps he really believed himself to be among troops on his own side. Whatever the cause of his strange behavior, he paid with his life for it.

Within weeks after the hanging of Major Andre, the entire Continental Army knew of the event, the British command was made aware of it, and in a detailed document Sir Henry Clinton explained what he had in mind in case Arnold would have been able to deliver West Point and its garrison to the British . . . Thus, the name Andre became a household word among the troops of both sides.

After his execution on October 2, 1780, at Tappan, Andre was buried at the foot of the gallows. In 1821 his body was exhumed and taken to England and reburied at Westminster Abbey. By 1853 tempers had sufficiently cooled and British-American friendship was firmly enough established to permit the erection of a monument to the event on the spot where the three militia men had come across Major Andre. On the occasion of the centennial of Andre's capture, a statue and bronze plaque were added and the monument surrounded with a protective metal fence. It stands near a major road and can easily be observed when passing by car. It is a beautiful monument, worthy of the occasion. There is only one thing wrong with it, be it ever so slight: *It stands at the wrong spot.* My good friend, Elliott Schryver, the eminent editor and scholar, pointed out the actual spot at some distance to the east.

In studying Harry Hansen's book on the area, I have the impression that he shares this view. In order to make a test of my own, we stopped by the present monument, and I asked Ingrid to tell me what she felt. I had purposely told her that the spot had no direct connection with anything else we were doing that day, so she could not consciously sense what the meaning of our brief stop was. Walking around the monument two or three times, touching it, and "taking in" the atmosphere psychically, she finally came up to me, shook her head, and said, "I am sorry, Hans, there is absolutely nothing here. Nothing at all."

But why not? If the Revolutionary taverns can be moved a considerable distance to make them more accessible to tourists, why shouldn't a momument be erected where everyone can see it instead of in some thicket where a prospective visitor might break a leg trying to find it? Nobody cares, least of all Major Andre.

# 2
# The "Conference House" Ghosts

Peace conferences and ghosts don't easily go together — unless we are talking about the one on Staten Island.

Peace conferences may go on for years and years without yielding tangible results — so it is a refreshing thought to remember that a peace conference held on Staten Island between Lord Howe, the British commander in America, and a Congressional committee consisting of Benjamin Franklin, John Adams, and Edward Rutledge lasted but a single day — September 11, 1776, to be exact.

The position was this: The British were already in command of New York, Long Island, and Staten Island, and the Yankees still held New Jersey and Pennsylvania, with Philadelphia as the seat of the Continental Congress. In view of his tremendous successes in the war against the colonists, Lord Howe felt that the suppression of the independence movement was only a matter of weeks. Wanting to avoid further bloodshed and also save himself some trouble, he suggested that a peace conference be held to determine whether an honorable peace could be concluded at that juncture of events.

Congress received his message with mixed emotions, having but lately worked out internal differences of opinion concerning the signing of the Declaration of Independence. A committee was appointed, consisting of the aforementioned three men and empowered to investigate the offer. The three legislators went by horse to Perth Amboy, New Jersey, and were met at the shore by a barge manned by British soldiers under a safe-conduct pass across the bay. They landed on the Staten Island shore and walked up to Bentley Manor, the residence of Lord Howe. There they were met with politeness and courtesies but also with a display of British might, for there were soldiers in full battle dress lined up along the road.

Later, the flamboyant John Adams told of soldiers "looking as fierce as ten furies, and making all the grimaces and gestures and motions of their muskets, with bayonets fixed, which, I suppose, military etiquette requires, but which we neither understood nor regarded."

Lord Howe outlined his plan for a settlement, explaining that it was futile for the Americans to carry on the war, and that the British were willing to offer peace with honor. Of course, any settlement would involve the colonies remaining under British rule. The three envoys listened in polite silence, after which Benjamin Franklin informed Lord

Howe that the Declaration of Independence had already been signed on July 4, 1776, and that they would never go back under British rule.

The conference broke up, and Lord Howe, still very polite, had the trio conveyed to Amboy in his own barge, under the safe-conduct pass he had granted them. The following day, September 12, 1776, the War of Independence entered a new round: The Yankees knew what the British government was willing to offer them in order to obtain peace, and they realized that they might very well win the war with just a little more effort. Far from discouraging them, the failure of the peace conference on Staten Island helped reinforce the Continental Congress in its determination to pursue the War of Independence to its very end.

This historical event took place in a manor house overlooking Raritan Bay. At the time, and for many years afterward, it was considered the most outstanding building on Staten Island. The two-story white building dates to before 1680 and is a colonial manor built along British lines. It was erected by a certain Christopher Billopp, a somewhat violent and hardheaded sea captain who had served in the British Navy for many years. Apparently, Captain Billopp had friends at court in London, and when the newly appointed Governor Andros came to America in 1674 he gave Billopp a patent as lieutenant of a company of soldiers. In the process, Billopp acquired nearly one thousand acres of choice land on Staten Island. But Billopp got into difficulties with his governor and re-entered navy service for awhile, returning to Staten Island under Governor Thomas Dongan. In 1677, he received a land grant for Bentley Manor, sixteen hundred acres of very choice land, and on this tract he built the present manor house. The Billopp family members were fierce Tories and stood with the Crown to the last. The Captain's grandson, also named Christopher, who was already born in the manor, lived there till the end of the Revolution, when he moved to New Brunswick, Canada, along with many other Tories who could not stay on in the newly independent colonies.

From then on, the manor house has had a mixed history of owners and gradually fell into disrepair. Had it not been built so solidly, with the keen eye of a navy man's perception of carpentry, perhaps none of it would stand today. As it was, an association was formed in 1920 to restore the historical landmark to its former glory. This has now been done, and the Conference House, as it is commonly called, is a museum open to the public. It is located in what was once Bentley Manor but today is called Tottenville, and it can easily be reached from New York City via the Staten Island Ferry. The ground floor contains two large rooms and a staircase leading to the upper story, which is also divided into two rooms. In the basement is a kitchen and a vault-like enclosure. Both basement and attic are of immense proportions. The large room downstairs to the left of the entrance was originally used as a dining room and the room to the right as a parlor. Upstairs, the large room to the left is a bedroom, while the one to the right is nowadays used as a Benjamin Franklin museum. In between the two large rooms is a small room, perhaps a child's room at one time. At one time there also was a tunnel from the vault in the basement to the water's edge, which was used as a means of escape during Indian attacks, a frequent occurrence in early Colonial days. Also, this secret tunnel could be used to obtain supplies by the sea route without being seen by observers on land.

As early as 1962 I was aware of the Conference House and its reputation of being haunted. My initial investigation turned up a lot of hearsay evidence, hardly of a scientific nature, but nevertheless of some historical significance inasmuch as there is usually a grain of truth in all legendary stories. According to the local legends, Captain Billopp had jilted his fiancée, and she had died of a broken heart in the house. As a result, strange noises, including murmurs, sighs, moans, and pleas of an unseen voice, were reported to have been heard in the house as far back as the mid-nineteenth century. According to the old Staten Island newspaper *The Transcript*, the phenomena were heard by a number of workmen during the restoration of the house after it had been taken over as a museum.

My first visit to the Conference House took place in 1962, in the company of Ethel Johnson Meyers and two of her friends, who had come along for the ride since they were interested in the work Mrs. Meyers and I were doing. Mrs. Meyers, of course, had no idea where we were going or why we were visiting Staten Island. Nevertheless, when we were still about a half-hour's ride away from the house, she volunteered her impressions of the place we were going to. When I encouraged her to speak freely, she said that the house she had yet to see was white, that the ground floor was divided into two rooms, and that the east room contained a brown table and eight chairs. She also stated that the room to the west of the entrance was the larger room of the two, and that some silverware was on display in that room.

When we arrived at the house, I checked these statements at once; they were entirely correct, except that the number of chairs was seven, not eight as Mrs. Meyers had stated. I questioned the resident curator about this seeming discrepancy. One of the chairs and the silverware had indeed been on display for years but had been removed from the room eight years prior to our visit.

"Butler," Mrs. Meyers mumbled as we entered the house. It turned out that the estate next to Bentley belonged to the Butlers; undoubtedly, members of that family had been in the Conference House many times. As is my custom, I allowed my medium free rein of her intuition. Mrs. Meyers decided to settle on the second-story room to the left of the staircase, where she sat down on the floor for want of a chair.

Gradually entering the vibrations of the place, she spoke of a woman named Jane whom she described as being stout, white-haired, and dressed in a dark green dress and a fringed shawl. Then the medium looked up at me and, as if she intuitively knew the importance of her statement, simply said, "Howe." This shook me up, since Mrs. Meyer's had no knowledge of Lord Howe's connection with the place she was in. I also found interesting Mrs. Meyer's description of a "presence," that is to say, a ghost, whom she described as a big man in a fur hat, being rather fat and wearing a skin coat and high boots, a brass-buckled belt, and black trousers. "I feel boats around him, nets, sailing boats, and I feel a broad foreign accent," Mrs. Meyers stated, adding that she saw him in a four-masted ship of a square-rigger type. At the same time she mentioned the letter T. What better description of the Tory, Captain Billopp, could she have given!

"I feel as if I am being dragged somewhere by Indians," Mrs. Meyers suddenly exclaimed, as I reported in my original account of this case in my first book *Ghost Hunter*. "There is violence, and somebody dies on a pyre of wood. Two men, one white, one Indian; and on two sticks nearby are their scalps." It seemed to me that what Mrs. Meyers had tuned in on were remnants of emotional turmoil in the early colonial days; as I have noted, Indian attacks were quite frequent during the early and middle parts of the eighteenth century.

When we went down into the cellar, Mrs. Meyers assured us that six people had been buried near the front wall during the Revolutionary War and that they were all British soldiers. She also said that eight more were buried somewhere else on the grounds, and she had the impression that the basement had been used as a hospital during an engagement. Later investigation confirmed that members of the Billopp family had been buried on the grounds near the road and that British soldiers might very well have been buried there, too, since there were frequent skirmishes around the house from July 1776, to the end of the year. Captain Billopp was twice kidnapped from his own house by armed bands operating from the New Jersey shore.

It was clear to me that Mrs. Meyers was entering various layers of history and giving us bits and pieces of her impressions, not necessarily in the right order but as she received them. The difficulty with trance mediumship is that you cannot direct it the way you want to, that is to say, ferret out just those entities or layers from the past you are interested in. You have to take "pot luck," as it were, hoping that sufficient material of interest will come through the medium.

Once more we returned to the upper part of the house. Suddenly, Mrs. Meyers turned white in the face and held on for dear life to the winding staircase. For a moment she seemed immobilized. Then, coming to life again, she slowly descended the stairs and pointed to a spot near the landing of the second story. "A woman was killed here with a crooked knife!" she said.

Aha, I thought, there is our legend about Captain Billopp and his jilted financée. But he didn't kill her; she had died of a broken heart. Mrs. Earley, the custodian, was trying to be helpful, so I questioned her about any murder that might have occurred in the house. "Why, yes," she obliged. "Captain Billopp once flew into a rage and killed a female slave on that very spot on the stairs." As she spoke, I had the impression that the custodian herself was shuddering just a little.

From time to time people had told me of their visits to the Conference House and wondered whether the "ghost in residence" was still active. Finally, I asked a young lady I had been working with for some time to try her hand at picking up whatever might be left in the atmosphere of the Conference House. Ingrid Beckman, an artist by profession, knew very little about the house but had access to the short account of my investigation given in *Ghost Hunter*.

I asked Ingrid to go to the house by herself, and on the afternoon of November 25, 1972, she paid a visit.

In order to avoid tourists, she arrived at the house about one o'clock. The house was still closed to visitors so she sat down on a bench outside. "I walked around, and even on the outside I felt a presence," Ingrid began her report to me. "I felt as if the place were really alive. Then I went up to the front porch and peeked into the main hallway, and when I looked up the stairs I had a feeling of gloom and foreboding. I had the distinct sensation of a dangerous situation there."

Strangely enough, Ingrid seemed to have been led to that house. Two weeks prior to her visit, she had happened to find herself in Nyack, New York, browsing through some antique shops. There she met a woman who started to talk to her. The woman explained that she was from Staten Island, and when she discovered that Ingrid lived there also, she suggested that Ingrid visit a certain house, once the property of an old sea captain. The house, the lady said, had an interesting tunnel which began behind a fireplace and ran down to the water's edge. Ingrid, always interested in visiting old houses, had promised to look into the matter. This was two weeks before I mentioned a visit to the Conference House to her.

The following weekend, Ingrid was with some friends at her apartment on Staten Island. She took the opportunity of asking whether any of them had ever heard of the house as described by her acquaintance. One of the young men present affirmed that there was such a house, called the Conference House, and that it was haunted by the spirit of a slave who had been killed there. That was on Sunday. The following Monday I telephoned Ingrid with the request to go to the Conference House.

As Ingrid was sitting on the front porch of the house waiting for the door to be opened, she had the distinct feeling that someone was watching her. "I felt as if someone knew I was there," she explained, "and I especially felt this coming from the window about the hallway. It is a crooked window, and I felt that it had some sort of significance. If anyone were looking at me or wanted to get my attention, it would be through that window. But when I went in, as soon as the door had been opened to visitors, the first place I went was the basement.

As I was looking around the basement, I came upon a little archway, as if I had been *directed* to go there."

The spot made her literally jump; she felt that something terrible had occurred near the fireplace, and she experienced heavy chills at the same time; someone had been brutalized at the entrance to the tunnel. Fortunately, she had managed to go there by herself, having discouraged the tourist guide from taking her around. "The tunnel entrance is particularly terrorizing," Ingrid said. "This tunnel caused me chills all the way up to my neck."

Finally tearing herself away from the basement, she went up the stairs, again by herself. Immediately she arrived at the upper landing and went to the bedroom to the left; as she stood in the entranceway, she heard a noise like a knock.

"The hallway upstairs felt terrible," Ingrid explained. "I turned around and looked down the stairs. As I looked, I almost became dizzy. It felt as if someone had been pushed down them or hurt on them." To be sure that she wasn't imagining things or being influenced by what she had read, Ingrid decided to go up and down those stairs several times. Each time, the sensation was the same. On one of her trips up the stairs, she ascertained that the window, which had so attracted her while she was still waiting outside, was indeed just outside the haunted stairwell.

"I got the impression of a slave woman, especially in the upstairs bedroom; I also felt there was a disturbance around the table downstairs, but I don't think the two are connected. I felt the woman was associated with the upstairs bedroom and the stairway and possibly the tunnel entrance; but the feeling in the basement is another episode, I think."

"What period do you think the disturbances go back to?" I asked.

"I'd say the 1700s, going back before the Revolution."

"Do you have the feeling that there is still something there that hasn't been fully resolved?"

"Yes, definitely. I think that is why I had such strong vibrations about it, and I think that is also why I got the information two weeks beforehand."

"Do you think that it is a man or a woman who is 'hung up' in there?"

"I think it is a woman, but there may also be a man because the scene at the table had something to do with a man. He may have been shot, or he may have been abducted from that room — you know, taken through the tunnel."

I suddenly recalled that Captain Billopp was twice abducted by Yankee irregulars from the Jersey shore. Gabriel Disosway, in his 1946 account of the Manor of Bentley, reported that "Colonel Billopp, at the time a warm party man and military leader, was closely watched, and, it is said, was twice taken from his own house by armed bands from 'the Jerseys,' and thus made a prisoner. Amboy is in sight, and upon one of these occasions, he was observed by some Americans, who had stationed themselves with a spy glass in the church steeple of that town. As soon as they saw him enter his abode, they ran to their boats, rapidly crossed the river, and he was soon their captive."

On January 28, 1973, Ingrid made another, spontaneous visit to the Conference House. She had much the same impressions as before, but this time she managed to speak to the caretaker. The lady admitted hearing heavy footsteps upstairs at times, which sounded to her like those of a man wearing heavy boots with spurs attached. Also, on the anniversary of the "the murder," the caretaker claims to have seen a man run up the stairs toward a girl waiting on the first landing. "Her story is that the girl was beheaded," Ingrid reported further. "She says that one afternoon last summer, as she was dusting the room on the left of the ground floor, she could put her hand 'right through' a British soldier! This past summer her daughter from South Carolina came to visit and insisted on staying upstairs in the haunted rooms. That night the daughter allegedly heard a man's laughter, followed by a woman's laughter, and then a shriek. According to the caretaker, this happens at regular intervals."

# 3
# The Hauntings at the White House

I thought it would be easy to get into the White House and ask about ghosts. Why, the president should be delighted to tell the world all about it. Not so! . . .

I don't think anyone has had more trouble getting into the White House for a specific purpose than I, except — perhaps — some presidential aspirants such as Thomas E. Dewey. Mr. Dewey's purpose was a lot easier to explain than mine, to begin with. How do you tell an official at the presidential mansion that you would like to go to the Lincoln Bedroom to see whether Lincoln's ghost is still there? How do you make it plain that you're not looking for sensationalism, that you're not bringing along a whole covey of newspaper people, all of which can only lead to unfavorable publicity for the inhabitants of the White House, whoever they may be at the time?

Naturally, this was the very difficult task to

which I had put myself several years ago. Originally, when I was collecting material for *Window to the Past*, I had envisioned myself going to the Lincoln Bedroom and possibly the East Room in the White House, hoping to verify and authenticate apparitions that had occurred to a number of people in those areas. But all my repeated requests for permission to visit the White House in the company of a reputable psychic were turned down. Even when I promised to submit my findings and the writings based on those findings to White House scrutiny prior to publication, I was told that my request could not be granted.

The first reason given was that it was not convenient because the president and his family were in. Then it was not convenient because they would be away. Once I was turned down because my visit could not be cleared sufficiently with Security, and anyway, that part of the White House I wanted to visit was private.

I never gave up. Deep down I had the feeling that the White House belongs to the people and is not a piece of real estate on which even the presidential family may hang out a sign, "No Trespassers." I still think so. However, I got nowhere as long as the Johnsons were in the White House.

I tried again when I started work on this account. A colonel stationed in the White House, whom I met through a mutual friend, Countess Gertrude d'Amecourt, tried hard to get permission for me to come and investigate. He, too, failed.

Next, I received a letter, quite unexpectedly,

from the Reverend Thomas W. Dettman of Niagara, Wisconsin. He knew a number of very prominent men in the federal government and offered to get me the permission I needed. These men, he explained, had handled government investigations for him before, and he was sure they would be happy to be of assistance if he asked them. He was even sure they would carry a lot of weight with the president. They knew him well, he asserted. Mr. Dettman had been associated with the Wisconsin Nixon for President Committee, and offered to help in any way he could.

After thanking Mr. Dettman for his offer, I heard nothing further for a time. Then he wrote to me again explaining that he had as yet not been able to get me into the Lincoln Bedroom, but that he was still working on it. He had asked the help of Representative John Byrnes of Wisconsin in the matter, and I would hear further about it. Then Mr. Dettman informed me that he had managed to arrange for me to be given "a special tour" of the White House and, to the best of his knowledge, that included the East Room. He then asked that I contact William E. Timmons, Assistant to the President, for details.

I was, of course, elated. Imagine, a special tour of the White House! What could be better than that?

With his letter, Mr. Dettman had included a letter from Senator William Proxmire of Wisconsin, in which the senator noted that I would not be able to do research in the Lincoln Bedroom, but that I would be given the special tour of the White House.

I hurriedly wrote a thank-you note to Mr. Dettman, and started to make plans to bring a medium to Washington with me. A few days later Mr. Dettman wrote me again.

He had received a call from the White House concerning the tour. He could, he explained, in no way guarantee what *kind* of tour I would be given, nor what I would see. He had done everything possible to help me and hoped I would not be disappointed.

Whether my own sixth sense was working or not, I suddenly thought I had better look into the nature of that "special tour" myself. I wrote and asked whether I would be permitted to spend half an hour in the East Room, since the Lincoln Bedroom had been denied me. Back came a letter dated May 14, 1970, on White House stationery, and signed by John S. Davies, Special Assistant to the President, Office White House Visitors.

*Senator Proxmire's recent letter to Mr. William Timmons concerning your most recent request to visit the White House has been referred to me, as this office is responsible for White House visitors. Unfortunately, as we have pointed out, we are unable to arrange for you to visit the Lincoln Bedroom, as this room is in the President's personal residence area, which is not open to visitors. If you wish to arrange an early-morning special tour, I suggest you contact Senator Proxmire's office. You are also most welcome to come to the White House any time during the regular visiting hours.*

I decided to telephone Mr. Davies since the day of my planned visit was close at hand. It was only then that I realized what that famous "special tour" really was. It meant that I, along with who else might be present at the time at the White House gates, would be permitted to walk through the part of the White House open to all visitors. I couldn't bring a tape recorder. I could not sit down or tarry along the way. I had to follow along with the group, glance up at whatever might be interesting, and be on my way again like a good little citizen. What, then, was so "special" about that tour, I inquired? Nothing really, I was told, but that is what it is known as. It is called a special tour because you have to have the request of either a senator or a representative from your home state.

I canceled my visit and dismissed the medium. But my reading public is large, and other offers to help me came my way.

Debbie Fitz is a teenage college student who wanted me to lecture at her school. In return, she offered to get me into the White House, or at least try to. I smiled at her courage, but told her to go right ahead and try. She wrote a letter to Miss Nixon, the president's daughter, whom she thought would be favorable to her request, being of the same age group and all that. After explaining her own interest in ESP research and the importance this field has in this day and age for the young, she went on to explain who I was and that I had previously been denied admittance to the White House areas I wished to do research in. She wrote:

*All he wants to do is take a psychic medium into the room and scientifically record any phenomena that may exist. This will not involve staying overnight; it can be done during the day at your convenience. All investigations are conducted in a scientific manner and are fully documented. It is well known that Lincoln himself was psychic and held séances in the White House. Wouldn't you, as a student of White House history and a member of the young, open-minded generation, like to find out whether or not this room is really haunted? This will also provide an opportunity for young people who are interested in other things besides riots and demonstrations to benefit intellectually from Mr. Holzer's efforts.*

Debbie Fitz never received a reply or an acknowledgment. I, of course, never heard about the matter again.

Try as I would, I was rebuffed. Just the same, interest in the haunted aspects of the nation's Executive Mansion remains at a high level. Several Washington newspapers carried stories featuring some of the psychic occurrences inside the White House, and whenever I appeared on Washington television, I was invariably asked about the ghosts at the White House. Perhaps the best account of the psychic state of affairs at number 1600 Pennsylvania Avenue was written by the *Washington Post* reporter, Jacqueline Lawrence.

"The most troubled spirit of 1600 Pennsylvania Avenue is Abraham Lincoln, who during his own lifetime claimed to receive regular visits from his two dead sons, Pat and Willie." After reporting the well-known premonitory dream in which Lincoln saw himself dead in a casket in the East Room, Miss Lawrence goes on to report that Mrs. Franklin Delano Roosevelt's servant, Mary Evan, had reported seeing Lincoln on the bed in the northwest bedroom, pulling on his boots. "Other servants said they had seen him lying quietly in his bed, and still others vowed that he periodically stood at the oval window over the main entrance of the White House. Mrs. Roosevelt herself never saw Lincoln, but she did admit that when working late she frequently felt a ghostly sort of presence."

Amongst the visitors to the White House who had experienced psychic occurrences was the late Queen Wilhelmina of the Netherlands. Asleep in the Queen's Bedroom, she heard someone knock at her door, got up, opened it, and saw the ghost of President Lincoln standing there looking at her. She fainted, and by the time she had come to he was gone.

"According to the legend, the spirit of Lincoln is especially troubled and restless on the eve of national calamities such as war." Under the circumstances, one should expect the shade of President Lincoln to be in around-the-clock attendance these days and nights.

But Lincoln is not the only ghost at the White House. Household members of President Taft have observed the ghost of Abigail Adams walking right through the closed doors of the East Room with her arms outstretched. And who knows what other specters reside in these ancient and troubled walls?

That all is not known about the White House may be seen from a dispatch of the *New York Daily News* dated November 25, 1969, concerning two new rooms unearthed at the White House. "Two hitherto unknown rooms, believed to date back to the time of Thomas Jefferson, have been unearthed in the White House a few yards away from the presidential swimming pool. The discovery was made as excavation continued on the larger work area for the White House press corps. The subterranean rooms, which White House curator James Ketchum described as storage or coal bins, were believed among the earliest built at the White House. Filled with dirt, they contained broken artifacts believed to date back to President Lincoln's administration."

When I discussed my difficulties in receiving permission for a White House investigation with prominent people in Washington, it was suggested to me that I turn my attention to Ford's Theatre or the Parker House — both places associated with the death of President Lincoln. I have not done so, for the simple reason that in my estimation the ghost of Lincoln is nowhere else to be found but where it mattered to him: in the White House. If there is a transitory impression left behind at Ford's Theatre, where he was shot, or the Parker House, where he eventually died some hours later, it would only be an imprint from the past. I am sure that the surviving personality of President Lincoln is to a degree attached to the White House because of unfinished business. I am sure that the disturbances at the White House have never ceased. Only a number of years ago, Lynda, one of the Johnson daughters, heard someone knock at her door, opened it, and found no one outside. Telephone calls have been put through to members of the presidential family, and there has been no one on the other end of the line. Moreover, on investigating, it was found that the White House operators had not rung the particular extensions.

It is very difficult to dismiss such occurrences as products of imagination, coincidence, or the "settling of an old house." Everyone knows the difference between human footsteps caused by feet encased with boots or shoes and the normal noises of an old house settling slowly and a little at a time on its foundation.

# 4
# A Ghost in Brooklyn

You wouldn't think that there are ghosts in such an ordinary, practical place like Brooklyn, New York — ghosts are supposed to be roaming British castles and dungeons.

But this ghost was in every way as interesting and challenging as some of those European "un-dead" haunting the ancient castles and palaces.

Clinton Street, Brooklyn, is one of the oldest sections of that borough, pleasantly middle class at one time, and still amongst Brooklyn's best neighborhoods, as neighborhoods go. The house in question is in the 300 block, and consists of four stories. There is a basement floor, then a parlor floor a few steps up, as is the usual custom with brownstone houses, with a third and fourth floor above it. If one preferred, one could call the third floor the fourth floor, in which case the basement becomes the first floor; but no matter how one called it, there were four levels in this brownstone, all capable of serving as apartments for those who wished to live there. The house was more than 100 years old at the time of the events herein described, and the records are somewhat dim beyond a certain point.

In the 1960s, the house was owned by some off-beat people, about whom little was known. Even the Hall of Records isn't of much help, as the owners didn't always live in the house, and the people who lived in it were not necessarily the owners. However, for the purpose of my story, we need only concern ourselves with the two top floors; the third floor contained two bedrooms and a bath, while the fourth or top floor consisted of a living room, dining room, kitchen, and second bath.

At the time my account begins, the first two floors were rented and only the two top floors were available for new tenants.

It was in the summer when two young ladies in their early twenties decided to find a place of their own. Somehow they heard of the two vacant floors in the house on Clinton Street and immediately fell in love with them, renting without much hesitation. Both Barbara and Sharon were still going to college and trying to make ends meet on what money they could manage between them. Two years later, Barbara was living in San Francisco with a business of her own, independently merchandising clothing. Brooklyn was only a hazy memory by then, but on August 1 of the year she and Sharon moved in, it was very much her world.

Immediately after moving in, they decided to clean up the house, which indeed needed it. The stairway was carpeted all the way up, and it was quite a job to vacuum it because there were a lot of outlets along the way, and one had to look out for extension cords. Sharon got to the top floor and was cleaning it when she removed the extension cord to plug it in further up. Instead, she just used the regular cord of the vacuum cleaner, which was about 12 feet long, using perhaps 3 feet of it, which left 9 feet of cord lying on the floor.

All of a sudden, the plug just pulled out of the wall. Sharon couldn't believe her eyes; the plug actually pulled itself out of the socket, and flew out onto the floor. She shook her head and put it back in, and turned the vacuum cleaner on again. Only then did she realize that she had turned the switch on the cleaner back on, when she had never actually turned it off in the first place! She couldn't figure out how that was possible. But she had a lot more work to do, so she continued with it. Later she came downstairs and described the incident to her roommate who thought she was out of her mind. "Wait till something happens to you," Sharon said. "There is something strange about this house."

During the next five months, the girls heard strange noises all over the house, but they attributed them to an old house settling, or the people living downstairs. Five months of "peace" were rudely shattered when Sharon's younger brother came to visit from New Jersey.

He was still in high school, and liked to listen to music at night, especially when it was played as loud as possible. The young people were sitting in the living room listening to music and talking. It was a nice, relaxed evening. All of a sudden the stereo went off. The music had been rather loud rock and roll, and at first they thought the volume had perhaps damaged the set. Then the hallway light went out, followed by the kitchen light. So they thought a fuse had blown. Barbara ran down four flights of stairs into the basement to check. No fuse had blown. To be on the safe side, she checked them anyway, and switched them around to make sure everything was fine. Then she went back upstairs and asked the others how the electricity was behaving.

But everything was still off. At this point, Sharon's brother decided to go into the kitchen and try the lights there. Possibly there was something wrong with the switches. He went into the hallway where there was an old Tiffany-type lamp hanging at the top of the stairway. It had gone off, too, and he tried to turn it on and nothing happened. He pulled again, and suddenly it went on. In other words, he turned it off first, then turned it on, so it had been on in the first place.

This rather bothered the young man, and he announced he was going into the kitchen to get something to eat. When he came back to join the others he was as white as the wall. He reported that the kitchen was as cold as an icebox, but as soon as one left the kitchen, the temperature was normal in the rest of the house. The others then got up to see for themselves, and sure enough, it was icy cold in the kitchen. This was despite the fact that there were four or five radiators going, and all the windows were closed.

That night they knew they had a ghost, and for want of a better name they called her Hendrix — it happened to have been the anniversary of Jimi Hendrix's death, and they had been playing some of his records.

Shortly afterward, Toby joined the other two girls in the house. Toby moved in on April 1. It had been relatively quiet between the incident in the kitchen and that day, but somehow Toby's arrival was also the beginning of a new aspect of the haunting.

About a week after Toby moved in, the girls were in the living room talking. It was about 11:00 at night, and they had dimmers on in the living room. Toby was sitting on the couch, and Barbara and some friends were sitting on the other side of the room, where all of a sudden she felt a chilly breeze pass by her. It didn't touch her, but she felt it nonetheless, and just then the lights started to dim back and forth, back and forth, and when she looked up, she actually saw the dial on the dimmer moving by itself. As yet, Toby knew nothing about the haunting, so she decided to say nothing to the others, having just moved in, and not wishing to have her new roommates think her weird.

But things kept happening night after night, usually after 11:00 when the two girls and their friends sat around talking. After a couple of weeks, she could not stand it any longer, and finally asked the others whether they could feel anything strange in the room. Barbara looked at Sharon, and a strange look passed between them; finally they decided to tell Toby about the haunting, and brought her up to date from the beginning of their tenancy in the house.

Almost every day there was something new to report: Cooking equipment would be missing, clothing would disappear, windows opened by themselves, garbage cans would be turned over by unseen hands. Throughout that period, there was the continued walking of an unseen person in the living room located directly over the third-floor bedroom. And the girls heard it at any hour of the night, and once in a while even during the day. Someone was walking back and forth, back and forth. They were loud, stomping footsteps, more like a woman's, but they sounded as if someone was very angry. Each time one of them went upstairs to check, they found absolutely nothing.

The girls held a conference and decided that they had a ghost, make no mistake about it. Toby offered to look into the matter, and perhaps find out what might have occurred at the house at an an earlier age. Barbara kept hearing an obscure whistling, not a real tune or song that could be recognized, but a human whistle nevertheless. Meanwhile, Toby heard of a course on parapsychology being given at New York University, and started to take an interest in books on the subject. But whenever there were people over to visit them and they stayed in the living room upstairs past eleven o'clock at night, the ghost would simply run them out of the room with all the tricks in her ghostly trade.

"She" would turn the stereo on and off, or make the lights go on and off. By now they were convinced it was a woman. There were heavy shutters from the floor to the ceiling, and frequently it appeared as if a wind were coming through them and they would clap together, as if the breeze was agitating them. Immediately after that, they heard footsteps walking away from them, and there was an uncomfortable feeling in the room, making it imperative to leave and go somewhere else, usually downstairs into one of the bedrooms.

As yet, no one had actually seen her. That June, Bruce, Toby's friend, moved into the house with her. They had the master bedroom, and off the bedroom was a bathroom. Since Barbara would frequently walk through in the middle of the night, they left the light on in the bathroom all night so that she would not trip over anything. That particular night in June, Toby was looking up, not at the ceiling, but at the wall, when suddenly she saw a girl looking at her.

It was just like an outline, like a shadow on the wall, but Toby could tell that she had long hair arranged in braids. Toby looked up at her and called the apparition to her boyfriend's attention, but by the time he had focused on it she had disappeared.

He simply did not believe her. Instead, he asked Toby to go upstairs to the kitchen and make him a sandwich. She wasn't up there for more than five or ten minutes when she returned to the bedroom and found her boyfriend hidden under the covers of the bed. When she asked him what was wrong, he would shake his head, and so she looked around the room, but could find nothing unusual. The only thing she noticed was that the bathroom door was now wide open. She assumed that her boyfriend had gone to the bathroom, but he shook his head and told her that he had not.

He had just been sitting on the bed, when all of a sudden he saw the handle on the door turn by itself, and the door open. When he saw that, he simply dove under the covers until Toby returned. From that moment on, he no longer laughed at her stories about a house ghost. The following night, Toby woke up at two o'clock in the morning. The television set had been left on and she went to shut it off, and when she got back into bed, she happened to glance at the same place on the wall where she had seen the apparition the night before. For a moment or two she saw the same outline of a girl, only this time she had the impression that the girl was smiling at her.

Two weeks after that, Toby and her boyfriend broke up, and this rather shook her. She had come back home one day and didn't know that he had left, then she found a note in which he explained his reasons for leaving, and that he would get in touch with her later. This very much upset her, so much so that her two roommates had to calm her down. Finally, the two other girls went upstairs and Toby was lying on the bed trying to compose herself.

In the quiet of the room, she suddenly heard someone sob a little and then a voice said, "Toby." Toby got up from bed and went to the bottom of the stairs and called up, demanding to know what Barbara wanted. But no one had called her. She went back to the room and lay down again. Just then she heard a voice saying "Toby" again and again. On checking, she found that no one had called out to her — no one of flesh and blood, that is.

Toby then realized who had been calling her, and she decided to talk to "Henny," her nickname for Hendrix. In a quiet voice, Toby said, "Henny, did you call me?" and then she heard the voice answer, "Calm down, don't take it so hard, it will be all right." It was a girl's voice, and yet there was no one to be seen. The time was about five o'clock in the afternoon, and since it was in June, the room was still fairly light.

Toby had hardly recovered from this experience when still another event took place. Sharon had moved out and another girl by the name of Madeline had moved in. One day her brother came to visit from Chicago, and he brought a friend along who had had some experience of a spiritual nature. His name was Joey, and both boys were about 20 or 21 years old.

Madeline and her brother were much interested in unexplained phenomena, and they brought a Ouija board to the house. On Saturday, December 19, while it was snowing outside and the atmosphere was just right for a séance, they decided to make contact with the unhappy ghost in the house. They went upstairs into the living room and sat down with the board. At first it was going to be a game, and they were asking silly questions of it such as who was going to marry whom, and other romantic fluff. But halfway through the session, they decided to try to contact the ghost in earnest. The three girls and Madeline's brother sat down on the floor with their knees touching, and put the board on top. Then they invited Henny to appear and talk to them if she was so inclined. They were prepared to pick up the indicator and place their hands on it so it could move to various letters on the board.

But before their hands ever touched it, the indicator took off by itself! It shot over to the word Yes on the board, as if to reassure them that communication was indeed desired. The four of them looked at each other dumbfounded, for they had seen only too clearly what had just transpired. By now, they were all somewhat scared. However, Toby decided that, since she was going to be interested in psychic research, she might as well ask the questions. She began asking why the ghostly girl was still attached to the house. Haltingly, word for word, Henny replied and told her sad story.

It was a slow process, since every word had to be spelled out letter by letter, but the young people didn't mind the passage of time — they wanted to know why Henny was with them. It appears that the house once belonged to her father, a medical doctor. Her name was Cesa Rist and she had lived in the house with her family. Unfortunately she had fallen in love with a boy and wanted to marry him but her father would not allow it. She had died in the house after an illness several months later.

Her body was taken to Denver, Colorado, and buried in the family plot. Cesa realized that her boyfriend was dead also, because this all happened a long time ago. Her reasons for staying on in the house were to find help; she wanted her remains to be buried near her lover's in New York.

"Do you like the people who live in this house?" "Yes," the ghost replied. "Will you appear to us?" "Cesa has," the ghost replied, and as if to emphasize this statement, there suddenly appeared the shadow of a cross on the kitchen wall, for which there was no possible source except, of course, from the parapsychological point of view.

The girls realized they did not have the means to go to Denver and exhume Cesa's remains and bring them to New York, and they told the ghost as much. "Is there anything else we can do to help you?"

"Contact Holzer," she said. By that time, of course, Toby had become familiar with my works, and decided to sit down and write me a letter, telling me of their problem. They could not continue with the Ouija board or anything else that night; they were all much too shaken up.

On Monday, Toby typed up the letter they had composed, and sent it to me. Since they were not sure the letter would reach me, they decided to do some independent checking concerning the background of the house and, if possible, try to locate some record of Cesa Rist. But they were unsuccessful, even at the Hall of Records, the events having apparently transpired at a time when records were not properly kept.

When I received the letter, I was just about to leave for Europe and would be gone two and a half months. I asked the girls to stay in touch with me and, after my return, I would look into the matter. After Toby had spoken to me on the telephone, she went back into the living room and sat down quietly. She then addressed Henny and told her she had contacted me, and that it would be a couple of months before I could come to the house because I had to go to Europe.

Barbara decided not to wait, however; one night she went upstairs to talk to Henny. She explained the situation to her, and why she was still hanging around the house; she explained that her agony was keeping Cesa in the house, and that she must let go of it in order to join her boyfriend in the Great Beyond. Above all, she should not be angry with *them* because it was their home now. Somehow Barbara felt that the ghost understood, and nothing happened, nothing frightening at all. Relieved, Barbara sat down in a chair facing the couch. She was just sitting there, wondering whether Henny really existed, or whether she was talking to thin air.

At that moment, an ethereal form entered the room and stood near the couch. It looked as if she was leaning on the arm of the couch or holding onto the side of it. She saw the outline of the head, and what looked like braids around the front of her chest. For half a minute she was there, and then she suddenly disappeared.

It looked to Barbara as if the girl had been five feet four inches, weighing perhaps 120 pounds. Stunned, Barbara sat there for another ten or fifteen minutes, trying to believe what she had seen. She then walked downstairs to try to sleep. But sleep would not come; she kept thinking about her experience.

At the time Sharon had left, they were interviewing potential roommates to replace her. One particularly unpleasant girl had come over and fallen in love with the house. Both Barbara and Toby didn't want her to move in, but she seemed all set to join them, so Toby decided to tell her about the ghost. She hoped it would stop the girl from moving in. As Toby delineated their experiences with Henny, the would-be roommate became more and more nervous.

All of a sudden there was a loud crash in the kitchen, and they went to check on it. The garbage can had turned itself over and all the garbage was spilled all over the kitchen, even though no one had been near it. The new girl took one look at this and ran out as fast as she could. She never came back.

But shortly afterward, Toby went on vacation to California. There, she made arrangements to move and found employment in the market research department of a large department store. Under the circumstances, the girls decided not to renew the lease, which was up in July, but to move to another apartment for a short period. That September, they moved to California. Under the circumstances, they did not contact me any further, and I assumed that matters had somehow been straightened out, or that there had been a change in their plans. It was not until a year later that we somehow met in California, and I could fill in the missing details of Henny's story.

On the last day of the girls' stay at the house on Clinton Street in Brooklyn, with the movers going in and out, Toby went back into the house for one more look and to say good-bye to Henny. She went up to the living room and said a simple good-bye, and hoped that Henny would be all right. But there was no answer, no feeling of a presence.

For awhile the house stood empty, then it was purchased by the father of an acquaintance of the girls. Through him, they heard of the new people who had moved in after the house was sold. One day when they had just been in the house for a few days, they returned to what they assumed was an empty house.

They found their kitchen flooded with water: There were two inches of water throughout the kitchen, yet they knew they had not left the water taps on. Why had Henny turned the water on and let it run? Perhaps Henny didn't like the new tenants, after all. But she had little choice, really. Being a ghost, she was tied to the house.

Following her friends to San Francisco was simply impossible, the way ghosts operate. And unless or until the new tenants on Clinton Street call for my services, there is really nothing I can do to help Henny.

# 5
# The Haunting at Glen Cove

Castles, palaces, even churches and, of course, cemeteries — those are places one expects to be haunted.

But an elegant, expensive school? Never mind. Schools can be as haunted as . . . Morgan Hall, for instance!

When Alice was born, her parents moved into an old house in Brooklyn that had the reputation of being strange. Alice was only a few months old when they left again, but during those months she would not be taken into her mother's bedroom without a fierce struggle — a behavior so markedly different from her otherwise "good" behavior as a baby that it could not help but be noticed by her parents. While her father had no interest in such matters, her mother soon connected the child's strange behavior with the other strange things in the house: the doors that would open by themselves, the footsteps, the strange drafts, especially in that bedroom little Alice hated so much.

When Alice was about twelve years old, and the family had moved from the old neighborhood into another house, she all of a sudden one day found herself thinking of her grandmother. Her grandparents lived a distance away upstate and there had been no recent contact with them.

"Grandmother is dead," Alice said to her mother, matter-of-factly. Her mother stared at her in disbelief. Hours later the telephone rang. Grandmother, who had been in excellent health, had suddenly passed away.

Her mother gave the girl a queer look but she had known of such gifts and realized her daughter, an only child, was something special. Within six months, the telephone rang twice more. The first time, Alice looked up and said, "Grandfather's dead."

And then, "Uncle's dead."

And they were.

While her father shook his head over all this "foolishness," her mother did not scoff at her daughter's powers. Especially after Alice had received a dream warning from her dead grandmother, advising her of an impending car accident. She was shown the exact location where it would happen, and told that if her mother were to sit in front she would be badly hurt, but if Alice were to change places with her, Alice would not be as badly hurt.

After the dream, without telling her mother her reasons, she insisted on changing places with her on the trip. Sure enough, the car was hit by another automobile. Had her mother been where Alice sat, she might not have reacted quickly enough and been badly hurt. But Alice was prepared and ducked — and received only a whiplash.

Afterward, she discussed all this with her mother. Her mother did not scoff, but asked what her grandmother who had given them warning had looked like in the vision.

"She had on a house dress and bedroom slippers," Alice replied. Her mother nodded. Although the grandmother had lost both legs due to diabetes, she had been buried with her favorite bedroom slippers in the coffin. Alice had never seen nor known this.

When she was seventeen, Alice had a strong urge to become a nun. She felt the world outside had little to offer and began to consider entering a convent. Perhaps this inclination was planted in her mind when she was a camp counselor for a Catholic school on Long Island. She liked the serenity of the place and the apparently quiet, contemplative life of the sisters.

On her very first visit to the convent, however, she felt uneasy. Morgan Hall is a magnificently appointed mansion in Glen Cove, Long Island, that had only been converted to religious purposes some years ago. Prior to that it was the Morgan estate with all that the name of that wealthy family implies. Nothing about it was either ugly or frightening in the least, and yet Alice felt immediately terrified when entering its high-ceilinged corridors.

As a prospective postulant, she had to visit the

place several times prior to being accepted, and on each occasion her uneasiness mounted.

But she ascribed these feelings to her lack of familiarity with the new place. One night, her uncle and grandfather appeared in a dream and told her that everything would be all right. She took this as an encouragement to pursue her religious plans and shortly after formally entered the convent.

She moved in just days before her eighteenth birthday, looking forward to a life totally different from that of her friends and schoolmates. The room she was assigned adjoined one of the cloisters, but at first she was alone in it as her future roommate was to arrive a week late. Thus she spent her first days at Morgan Hall alone in the room. The very first night, after she had retired, she heard someone walking up and down outside the door. She thought this strange at that hour of the night, knowing full well that convents like their people to retire early. Finally her curiosity overcame her natural shyness of being in a new place, and she peeked out of her door into the corridor. The footsteps were still audible. But there was no one walking about outside. Quickly, she closed the door and went to bed.

The next morning, she discussed the matter with six other postulants in rooms nearby. They, too, had heard the footsteps that night. In fact, they had heard them on many other nights as well when there was positively no one walking about outside.

As she got used to convent routine, Alice realized how impossible it would be for one of them — or even one of the novices, who had been there a little longer than they — to walk around the place at the hour of the night when she heard the steps. Rigid convent rules included a 10 P.M. bell. Everybody had to be in bed at that time, except for dire emergencies. One just didn't walk about the corridors at midnight or later for the sheer fun of it at Morgan Hall, if she did not wish to be expelled. All lights go out at ten also, and nothing moves.

At first, Alice thought the novices were playing tricks on the new arrivals by walking around downstairs to create the footsteps, perhaps to frighten the postulants in the way college freshmen are often hazed by their elder colleagues. But she soon realized that this was not so, that the novices were no more allowed out after ten than they were.

Her psychic past did not allow Alice to let matters rest, and curiosity forced her to further inquire as best she could under the circumstances. After all, you don't run to the Mother Superior and ask, Who walks the corridors at night, Ma'am?

It was then she learned that the house had been J. P. Morgan's mansion originally and later had been used by the Russian Embassy. She recalled the battles the Russians had fought with the Glen Cove township over taxes and how they finally vacated the premises in less than perfect condition. As a sort of anticlimax, the Catholic nuns had moved in and turned the Hall into a convent and school.

A conversation with the convent librarian wasn't particularly fruitful, either. Yes, Mr. Morgan built the house in 1910. No, he didn't die here, he died in Spain. Why did she want to know?

Alice wondered about Mr. Morgan's daughter.

Alice Morgan had lived in this house and died here of typhoid fever in the early years of her life.

But try as she might, she never got the librarian to tell her anything helpful. Naturally, Alice did not wish to bring up the real reason for her curiosity. But it seemed as if the librarian sensed something about it, for she curtly turned her head sideways when speaking of the Morgans as if she did not wish to answer.

Frustrated in her inquiry, Alice returned to her chores. One night in October of 1965, Alice was walking in the hall of the postulancy, that part of the building reserved for the new girls who were serving their apprenticeship prior to being admitted to the convent and to taking their final vows.

It was a cool night, and Alice had walked fairly briskly to the extreme end of the hall and then stopped for a moment to rest. As she turned around and faced toward the opposite end of the hall, whence she had just come, she noticed a girl standing there who had not been there before. She wore a long, black dress similar to the dresses the postulants wore, and Alice took her to be her roommate.

She noticed the figure enter the room at the end of the hall. This room was not a bedroom but used by the postulants for study purposes.

It's Vera, Alice thought, and decided to join her and see what she was up to in that room.

Quickly she walked toward the room and entered it. The lights were off, and Alice thought this peculiar. Was her friend perhaps playing games with her? The room at this hour was quite dark.

So she turned on the lights and looked around. There was no one in the room now, and there was no way anyone could have left the room without her noticing it, Alice reasoned. She examined the windows and found them tightly closed. Not that she expected her friend to exit the room that way, but she wanted to be sure the person — whoever she might have been — could not have left that way. This was on the third floor, and anyone trying to leave by the windows would have had to jump or have a ladder outside.

Suddenly it hit Alice that she had not heard anything at all. All the time she had seen the figure walk into the room, there had been no footsteps, no noise of a door opening, nothing. Morgan Hall's doors open with a fair amount of squeaking, and none of that was audible when she had seen the figure.

Alice quickly left and hurried to her own room to figure this out quietly.

On recollection, she visualized the figure again and it occurred to her at once that there was something very odd about the girl. For one thing, the long gown the postulants wear moves when they walk. But the figure she had seen was stiff and seemed to glide along the floor rather than actually walk on it. The corridor was properly lit and she had seen the figure quite clearly. What she had not seen were her ankles and socks, something she would have observed had it been one of her friends.

Although the door was not closed, the room was

actually a corner room that could be entered in only one way, from the front door. Alice was sure she had not seen the figure emerge from it again. There was no place to hide in the room, had this been her roommate playing a joke on her. Alice had quickly examined the closet, desk, and beds — and no one was hiding anywhere in that room.

Eventually, she gathered up enough courage to seek out her friend Vera and discuss the matter with her. She found that there was a "joke" going around the convent that Alice Morgan's ghost was roaming the corridors, but that the whole matter was to be treated strictly as a gag. Yet she also discovered that there was one part of the Hall that was off limits to anyone *alone*. In what the girls called the catacombs, at ground level, was the laundry room. The third section, way back, was never to be entered by any of them at night, and in the daytime only if in pairs. Yet, the area was well lit. Alice could not get any information for the reasons for this strange and forbidding order. In a convent, speaking to anyone but one's own group is extremely difficult without "proper permission" and this was not a fitting subject to discuss.

The novices, whom she approached next, suddenly became serious and told her to forget it: There were things going on in the building that could not be explained. She was not to pay attention, and pray hard instead.

Alice wondered about this attitude, and perhaps it was then her first doubts concerning her ecclesiastical future began to enter her mind.

Shortly after (it was still October 1965) she lay awake in bed at night, thinking of her future at the convent. The clock had just chimed eleven and she was still wide awake. Night after night, she had heard the walking in the hall. After weeks of these manifestations, her nerves began to get edgy and she could not sleep as easily as she used to when she still lived in Brooklyn. Sure enough, there they were again, those incessant footsteps. They seemed to her the steps of a medium-heavy person, more like a woman's than a man's, and they seemed to be bent on some definite business, scurrying along the hall as if in a hurry.

Suddenly the night was pierced by a shriek: It seemed directly outside her door, but below. Since she was on the top floor, the person would have to be on the second floor.

There was no mistaking it, this was the outcry of a woman in great pain, in the agony of being hurt by someone!

This time she was almost too scared to look, but she did open the door only to find the corridor abandoned and quiet now.

She ran in to speak to the other postulants, regulations or no regulations. She found them huddled in their beds in abject fear. All eight of them had heard the bloodcurdling scream!

By now Alice was convinced that something strange had taken place here and that a restless personality was stalking the corridors. A short time later, she and Vera were in their room getting ready to retire.

It was a cold night, but no wind was about. The windows were the French type that locked with a heavy iron rod from top to bottom. No one could open the window from the outside, the only way it could be opened would be from the inside, by pushing the rod up.

"We don't have to lock the window tonight, do we?" Vera asked. "It isn't windy."

But they decided to do it anyway, as they did every night. They put their shoes on the window sill, something they were in the habit of doing frequently so that the small draft coming in below would "air them out."

After the window was locked, they retired.

It was well into the night when the girls awoke to a loud noise. The French window had broken open by itself and the shoes had been tossed inside the room as if by a strong storm!

They checked and found the air outside totally still. Whatever had burst their window open had not been the wind. But what was it?

The room was ice cold now. They shuddered and went back to bed.

There is only a small ledge, for pigeons to sit on outside the window, so no one could have opened it from that vantage point and one could hardly expect pigeons to burst a window open.

The girls then realized that the novices who had been complaining about the windows in their room being constantly open had not been fibbing. Alice and Vera always kept their windows closed, yet some unseen force had apparently opened them from inside on a number of occasions. Now they had seen for themselves how it happened.

Alice realized that the window had been broken open as if by force from *inside*, not outside.

"Someone's trying to get out, not in," she said, and her roommate could only shudder.

There were other peculiar things she soon noticed. Strange cold drafts upstairs and in the attic. Crosses nailed to the wall next to the entrance to the upstairs rooms. Only to those rooms, and to no others, and not inside the rooms, as one might expect in a convent, but just outside as if they had been placed there to keep something, or someone, evil out!

In the main dining room, a door, when closed, could not be distinguished from the wall. A trick window near the table was actually a mirror that allowed the man at the head of the table to see who was coming towards him from all sides.

Banker Morgan lived in considerable fear of his life, whether imagined or real, but certainly the house was built to his specifications. In fact, trick mirrors were so placed in various parts of the main house so that no one could approach from downstairs and surprise anyone upstairs, yet no one could detect anyone watching through them.

Shortly after Alice had moved into the convent, she began to have strange dreams in which a blonde young girl named Alice played a prominent role.

In the dream, the girl's blonde hair changed to curls, and Alice heard a voice say, "This is Alice Morgan, I want to introduce you to her."

But when she woke up, Alice thought this was only due to her having discussed the matter with the novices. Alice Morgan was not the disturbed person there, her psychic sense told her.

To her, all ghostly activities centered around that attic. There were two steps that always squeaked peculiarly when someone stepped on them. Many times she would hear them squeak and look to see who was walking on them, only to find herself staring into nothingness. This was in the daytime. On other occasions, when she was at work cleaning garbage cans downstairs — postulants do a lot of ordinary kitchen work — she would feel herself observed closely by a pair of eyes staring down at her from the attic. Yet, no one was up there then.

The torture of the nightly footsteps together with her doubts about her own calling prompted her finally to seek release from the convent and return to the outside world after three months as a postulant. After she had made this difficult decision, she felt almost as if all the burdens had lifted from the room that had been the center of the psychic manifestations.

She decided to make some final inquiries prior to leaving and, since her superiors would not tell her, she looked the place over by herself, talked to those who were willing to talk, and otherwise used her powers of observation. Surely, if the haunted area was upstairs — and she knew by now that it was — it could not be Alice Morgan who was the restless one.

But then who was?

The rooms on the third floor had originally been servant quarters, as is customary in the mansions of the pre-World War I period. They were built to house the usually large staffs of the owners. In the case of the Morgans, that staff was even larger than most wealthy families.

Was the "restless one" one of the maids who had jumped out the window in a final burst for freedom, freedom from some horrible fate?

Then her thoughts turned to the Communist Russian occupancy of the building. Had they perhaps tortured someone up there in her room? The thought was melodramatically tempting, but she dismissed it immediately. The figure she had seen in the hall was dressed in the long dress of an earlier period. She belonged to the time when the Morgan Hall was a mansion.

No, she reasoned, it must have been a young girl who died there while the Morgans had the place and perhaps her death was hushed up and she wanted it known. Was it suicide, and did she feel in a kind of personal hell because of it, especially now that the place was a convent?

Somehow Alice felt that she had stumbled upon the right answers. That night, the last night she was to spend at the convent prior to going home, she slept soundly.

For the first time in three months, there were no footsteps outside her door.

She waited for a while once the ten o'clock bell had sounded, but nothing happened. Whoever it was had stopped walking.

# 6
# The Ghostly Usher

Sometimes unfinished business, or old habits, or just confusion keeps someone bound to his former house or workplace — especially if the job meant a great deal to them.

So it was with the ghostly usher of Minneapolis.

For this account, I am indebted to a twenty-two-year-old creative production assistant in a Minneapolis advertising agency, by the name of Deborah Turner. Miss Turner got hooked on some of my books and started to look around the Twin Cities for cases that might whet my appetite for ghost hunting. Being musically inclined with an interest in theater, it was natural that she should gravitate toward the famed Guthrie Theater, named after the famous director, which is justly known as the pride of Minneapolis. At the theater she met some other young people, also in their early twenties, and shared her interest in psychic phenomena with them. Imagine her surprise when she discovered that she had stumbled upon a most interesting case.

Richard Miller was born in Manhattan, Kansas, in 1951. Until age ten, he lived there with his father, a chemist in government service. Then his father was transferred to England, and Richard spent several years going to school in that country. After that, he and his family returned to the United States and moved to Edina. This left Richard not only with a vivid recollection of England, but also with somewhat of an accent which, together with his childhood in Kansas, gave him a somewhat unusual personality.

His strange accent became the subject of ridicule by other students at Edina Morningside High School, and it did not go down well with the shy, introspective young man. In the tenth grade at this school, he made friends with another young man, Fred Koivumaki, and a good and close relationship sprang up between the two boys. It gave Fred a chance to get to know Richard better than most of the other fellows in school.

As if the strange accent were not enough to make him stand out from the other boys in the area, Richard was given to sudden, jerky movements, which made him a good target for sly remarks and jokes of his fellow students. The Millers did not have much of a social life, since they also did not quite fit into the pattern of life in the small town of Edina.

During the years spent in an English school, Richard had known corporal punishment, since it is still part of the system in some English schools. This terrified him, and perhaps contributed toward his inability to express himself fully and freely. Somehow he never acquired a girlfriend as the other students did, and this, too, bothered him a lot. He couldn't for the world understand why people didn't like him more, and often talked about it with his friend Fred.

When both young men reached the age of sixteen, they went to the Guthrie Theater where they got jobs as ushers. They worked at it for two years. Richard Miller got along well with the other ushers, but developed a close friendship only with Fred Koivumaki and another fellow, Barry Peterson. It is perhaps a strange quirk of fate that both Richard Miller and Barry Peterson never reached manhood, but died violently long before their time.

However, Richard's parents decided he should go to the university and quit his job. In order to oblige his parents, Richard Miller gave up the job as usher and moved into Territorial Hall for his first year at the university.

However, the change did not increase his ability to express himself or to have a good social life. Also, he seemed to have felt that he was catering to his parents' wishes, and became more antagonistic toward them. Then, too, it appears that these students also made him the butt of their jokes. Coincidentally, he developed a vision problem, with cells breaking off his retinas and floating in the inner humor of the eye. This caused him to see spots before his eyes, a condition for which there is no cure. However, he enjoyed skiing because he knew how to do it well, and joined the university ski club.

But Richard's bad luck somehow was still with him. On a trip to Colorado, he ran into a tree, luckily breaking only his skis. When summer came to the area, Richard rode his bike down a large dirt hill into rough ground and tall weeds at the bottom, injuring himself in the process. Fortunately, a motorcyclist came by just then, and got Richard to the emergency ward of a nearby hospital. All this may have contributed toward an ultimate breakdown; or, as the students would call it, Richard just "flipped out."

He was hospitalized at the university hospital and was allowed home only on weekends. During that time he was on strong medication but, when the medication did not improve his condition, the doctor took him off it and sent him home.

The following February 4, he decided to try skiing again, and asked his father to take him out to Buck Hill, one of the skiing areas not far from town. But to his dismay Richard discovered that he couldn't ski anymore, and this really depressed him. When he got home, there was a form letter waiting for him from the university, advising him that because he had skipped all the final exams due to his emotional problems at the time, he had received F's in all his classes and was on probation.

All this seemed too much for him. He asked his mother for forty dollars, ostensibly to buy himself new ski boots. Then he drove down to Sears on Lake Street, where he bought a high-powered pistol and shells. That was on Saturday, and he killed himself in the car. He wasn't found until Monday morning, when the lot-clearing crew found his body.

Richard Miller was given a quiet burial in Fort Snelling National Cemetery. His parents, Dr. and Mrs. Byron S. Miller, requested that donations to the Minnesota Association for Mental Health be sent instead of flowers. Richard's mother had always felt that her son's best years had been spent as an usher at the Guthrie Theater; consequently he was cremated wearing his Guthrie Theater blazer. The date was February 7, and soon enough the shock of the young man's untimely death wore off and only his immediate family and the few friends he had made remembered Richard Miller.

A few weeks after the death of the young usher, a woman seated in the theater in an aisle seat came up to the usher in charge of this aisle and asked him to stop the other usher from walking up and down during the play. The usher in charge was shocked, since he had been at the top of the aisle and had seen no one walk up and down. All the other ushers were busy in their respective aisles. However, the lady insisted that she had seen this young man walk up and down the aisle during the play. The usher in charge asked her to describe what she had seen. She described Richard Miller, even to the mole on his cheek. The incident is on record with the Guthrie Theater. Minneapolis Tribune columnist Robert T. Smith interviewed Craig Scherfenberg, director of audience development at the theater, concerning the incident. "There was no one in our employ at the time who fit the description," the director said, "but it fit the dead young man perfectly."

In the summer several years later, two ushers were asked to spend the night in the theater to make sure some troublesome air-conditioning equipment was fully repaired. The Guthrie Theater has a thrust stage with openings onto the stage on all three sides; these openings lead to an actors' waiting area, which in turn has a door opening onto an area used as a lounge during intermissions.

The two young men were sitting in this waiting area with both doors open, and they were the only people in the building. At one o'clock in the morning, they suddenly heard the piano onstage begin to play. Stunned by this, they watched in silence when they saw a cloudlike form floating through the lounge door and hovering in the center of the room. One of the ushers thought the form was staring at him. As quickly as they could gather their wits they left the room.

One of Deborah Turner's friends had worked late one evening shortly after this incident, repairing costumes needed for the next day's performance. She and a friend were relaxing in the stage area while waiting for a ride home. As she glanced into the house, she noticed that the lights on the aisle that had been the dead usher's were going on and off, as if someone were walking slowly up and down. She went to the ladies' room a little later, and suddenly she heard pounding on one wall, eventually circling the room and causing her great anxiety, since she knew that she and her friend were the only people in the house.

When the Guthrie Theater put on a performance of *Julius Caesar*, one of the extras was an older woman by the name of Mary Parez. She freely admitted that she was psychic and had been able to communicate with her dead sister. She told her fellow actors that she could sense Richard Miller's presence in the auditorium. Somehow she thought that the ghost would make himself known during Mark Antony's famous speech to the Romans after Caesar's death.

The scene was lit primarily by torches when the body of Julius Caesar was brought upon the stage. Jason Harlen, a young usher, and one of his colleagues were watching the performance from different vantage points in the theater. One boy was in one of the tunnels leading to the stage, the other in the audience. Both had been told of Mary Parez's prediction, but were disappointed when nothing happened at that time. In boredom, they began to look around the theater. Independently of each other they saw smoke rising to the ceiling and shaping itself into a human form. Both young men said that the form had human eyes.

The aisle that the late Richard Miller worked was number eighteen. Two women in the acting company of *Julius Caesar*, named Terry and Gigi, complained that they had much trouble with the door at the top of aisle eighteen for no apparent reason. Bruce Benson, who now worked aisle eighteen, said that people complained of an usher walking up and down the aisle during performances. Bruce Margolis, who works the stage door, leaves the building after everyone else. When he was there one night all alone, the elevator began running on its own.

All this talk about a ghost induced some of the young ushers to try and make contact with him via the Ouija board. Dan Burg, head usher, took a board with him to the stage and, along with colleagues Bruce Benson and Scott Hurner, tried to communicate with the ghost. For awhile nothing happened. Then, all of a sudden the board spelled, TIPTOE TO THE TECH ROOM. When they asked why, the board spelled, GHOST. They wanted to know which tech room the ghost was referring to: DOWNSTAIRS? NO, the communicator informed them. UPSTAIRS. The the board signed off with the initials MIL. At that, one of the men tipped over the board and wanted nothing further to do with it.

In November of the next year, an usher working at the theater told columnist Robert Smith, "It was after a night performance. Everyone had left the theater but me. I had forgotten my gloves and returned to retrieve them. I glanced into the theater and saw an usher standing in one of the aisles. It was him. He saw me and left. I went around to that aisle and couldn't find anything."

There is also an opera company connected with the Guthrie Theater. One night not long ago, one of the ladies working for the opera company was driving home from the Guthrie Theater. Suddenly she felt a presence beside her in the car. Terrified, she looked around and became aware of a young man with dark curly hair, glasses, and a mole on his face. He wore a blue coat with something red on the pocket — the Guthrie Theater blazer. With a sinking feeling, she realized that she was looking at the ghost of Richard Miller.

For the past two years, however, no new reports have come in concerning the unfortunate young man. Could it be that he has finally realized that there await him greater opportunities in the next dimension, and though his life on Earth was not very successful, his passing into the spiritual life might give him most of the opportunities his life on Earth had denied him? At any rate, things have now quieted down in aisle eighteen at the Guthrie Theater in Minneapolis, Minnesota.

# 7
# The Belleville Ghost

The quiet, often-conservative Middle West has had its share of tragedies and unsolved mysteries from the past. And its share of hauntings.

Belleville, Illinois, is a sleepy town about an hour's drive from St. Louis and has nothing particular to offer in the way of commerce or beauty, except for a few charming old houses still standing. The people who live in Belleville are seldom troubled by the controversies of the day and the industrial strife of nearby East St. Louis.

On Main Street near 17th there is an old brick house which has stood the test of time well: Built 125 years ago by a coal miner named Meyer, it has since been remodeled and also been added to, but the original structure is still sound and no one thinks of tearing it down or replacing it with something more up-to-date.

The house consists of two stories, with the front parlor well lit by large windows looking onto Main

Street. There are four rooms downstairs, a kitchen, and a hallway leading to the second section of the house which in turn leads to a small backyard. The house stands near the corner and is accessible from downtown in a matter of minutes. Eventually, it had passed out of the Meyer family into other hands, and its history is obscure until it became the property of a certain Mr. and Mrs. Joseph Stricker. Little else is known about them but their names. After they passed on, the house was acquired by two young sisters, Dollie and Judy Walta, who bought it not as living quarters, but in order to turn the place into studios for their music business. The Walta girls are music teachers. Dollie, born in 1929, and Judy, born in 1939, were two of ten children of Fred and Julia Walta, who had come to America from Czechoslovakia while still young. They gave their family a good education, but Judy rebelled against the strict discipline of school and quit after two years of high school. This despite an IQ of 134.

At sixteen, she was already an accomplished musician and decided to devote her life to the teaching of music. To this day she is a teacher of piano. Dollie, the elder sister, teaches guitar, and jointly they have operated a music studio in the house for the past eleven years. They go there every day except on weekends, and generally leave by 9 P.M. or earlier, depending on how many pupils they have that day. Once in a while, they have also come in on Saturday mornings.

At other times and at night, the house is deserted and well-locked up, and the chance of burglars breaking in is small due to its solid construction and the fact that it is on Main Street, usually well-patrolled by the local police department.

For the first six years of their tenancy, the sisters noticed nothing out of the ordinary in the old house. True, there were the usual squeaking floorboards and the aching sounds of an old house settling on its foundations. But that was to be expected, and no one paid any heed to such things. In 1962, they decided to make some alterations in the house to make the layout more suitable to their needs. Shortly after, Judy Walta had to come in late one night because she had forgotten to leave one of the inner doors unlocked so the cleaning woman could get in there in the morning.

She entered from the rear door, which leads to 17th Street, and did not bother to turn on any lights since the door she wanted to unlock was only a few steps beyond the back door. Swiftly, she unlocked it and then turned around to leave again. As she did so, she passed a white, misty figure in the hall. There was no mistaking it for anything else, and the whole incident took her so by surprise, she just backed away from it and out the rear door.

The next morning, she discussed the matter with her sister and, as nothing further happened out of the ordinary, they dropped the subject.

One of their students, a young man by the name of Jim Bawling, had been unhappy at his home and gotten into the habit of spending a great amount of time in their studio. In fact, it had gotten to be a kind of "home away from home" to him, and he became genuinely attached to the place and the sisters. Almost every afternoon he would come in and chat with them, whenever they were free to do so.

Eventually, he joined the Navy, and on his first leave, he returned to Belleville for a visit. On August 26, 1962, the young man drowned in an accident. On August 30, the day after his funeral, the sisters were in the room used for lessons when a pencil, which had been his and which he had left on his desk on his very last visit, started to roll off the desk, bounced on the eraser and dropped — pointing to the chair which had been his last seat!

There was no one close to the desk at the time, nor was there any movement or vibration outside the house. Moreover, the room is built on a slant and the pencil rolled *against* the slant.

Shortly after this incident, the sisters and many of their students began hearing the back door open by itself and close again. This was immediately followed by footsteps of someone walking through the hall. At first, they would get up to see who it was, but there was never anyone to be seen. Gradually, they realized that these were not the footsteps of a living person. The visitor would come at various times of the day or evening, and then stay away for several months. Then it would all resume. The sisters became used to these sounds, and hardly looked up when they became audible. One day the steps continued and then they could clearly hear someone sit down in the sailor's old chair!

It was clear to them that Jim was trying to make himself felt and wanted to continue his old friendship with them from where he now was. This did not bother them, but it bothered some of their pupils who held less broadminded views of ghosts.

The sisters were sure it was Jim, for that was his chair, and he always came in through the rear door rather than the front entrance.

The footsteps continued, and the door would still open and close by itself. Judy would just nod, and Dollie would say "Hello, Jim" and go on with her work.

But it soon became apparent to Dollie that the footsteps were not always the same: Sometimes they were soft and light, as if made by a young person, while at other times they were the heavy, almost clumsy steps of a big man.

On March 25, 1966, the two young women were in different parts of the studio busy with their chores. Judy was in the middle room, while Dollie was in the bathroom, with the door open. The time was 1:20 P.M. Independently of each other, the two girls saw the same figure of a man suddenly appear out of nowhere. At first, Judy saw him. He was a big man, about 5 feet 11 inches tall, and heavy-set, dressed in gray; and where his face should have been there was just a gray mass. But unmistakably this was a human figure. Thirty seconds later, he appeared to Dollie. She looked at him, and could see right through him into the other room!

The girls both had the impression that the man was looking *at them*. As he disappeared toward the rear of the house, they realized they had not heard a single sound. Naturally, they knew this was not

Jim, their erstwhile pupil. But who was it?

Since the appearance of the man in gray, the footsteps were not heard again, but the door kept opening and closing as before. Word of their strange house got around, and though they did not exactly cherish the notion, their pupils began to discuss the phenomena with them.

One young man whose work in the police had trained him to be a particularly competent observer of details, came forward to tell of a strange encounter on May 26 of that year. He was in the downstairs studio room at about 8 P.M. when he suddenly came face to face with a man in gray. He took him to be about thirty years of age and, just like the sisters, he could not make out any facial characteristics. It was almost as if the man did not want his face to be recognized and was hiding it in a blur.

One Saturday, Judy had come to make sure the building was properly locked. This was August 27, 1966, and between 3 and 3:30 P.M., she observed in the empty building the snapping of door locks, and a footstep — just one footstep — near the door leading from the hall into the basement of the house. This was immediately followed by the sound of several objects falling to the floor, although nothing was moving. One sound in particular reminded her of the noise made by dropping a small package to the floor, *or the muffled sound of a silencer on a gun*, she thought, with a shudder. What was she thinking? This seemed like a bad melodrama by now.

All this activity began to get on her nerves. The

following Tuesday, August 30, the two young women had their friends Rita Schulte and Mike Tolan in the house. It was after teaching hours, and the foursome was just sitting around relaxing. Rita had been taking piano lessons for the past year and was familiar with the "problems" of the house, but Mike laughed at it all, especially the man in gray. "You and your ghosts," he chortled. "It's all in your minds."

At that moment, the toilet was being flushed violently. They looked at each other. Everybody was accounted for and the toilet could not flush by itself. Mike tried and tried to see whether it might accidentally have done so. But it couldn't have. His face took on a more thoughtful mien as he sat down again.

A drum teacher named Dick P., working out of the studio, often told of the same noises — the back door opening and closing and the footsteps of an unseen visitor coming up and stopping inside the house. He knew from the sisters that there had never been anything unusual observed upstairs. He also knew the house was locked up tight and empty. But to his surprise, the upper story was lit up as if someone were up there. No reflection from passing cars could account for this. He drove on.

Jack McCormick is a clerk for the Internal Revenue Service, an outfit with little use for ghosts, since they don't pay taxes. His son has been studying with the Walta sisters for the past year and a half, and it was and is his custom to wait for him in the downstairs waiting room. He, too, has been constantly unnerved by the sound of the door opening and closing and the footsteps of someone not appearing.

Joe Bauer, a freight handler for the railroad, has heard the heavy footfalls of a man coming in the rear door, only to find no one there. Mrs. Bauer takes two lessons a week, and he often stays with her until about eight or nine in the evening. Everyone gets hungry by that time, so one of them would run out for hamburgers. One night while they — the two sisters and the Bauers — were eating and watching TV, Mrs. Bauer felt an icy hand on her back. She felt each and every finger but, when she shook herself and turned around, she saw that no one was near her. Needless to say, it did not help her appetite.

A little while after, all four saw the umbrella, which had been standing idly and quietly in its stand, move by its own volition. One of the sisters got up and stopped it. But the umbrella would not obey. A few moments later, it started swinging again. At the same time, the back door opened and closed with a bang. Everyone was out of the house faster than you can say "ghost" that evening.

The sisters decided that something had to be done about the power frightening them in the house. First, the house itself deserved to be carefully scrutinized. It was then they discovered that it actually consisted of three separate units, with the front section, where today's main entrance is, constructed at a later date than the rear. The original entrance had been to the rear, and what was the entrance at the time the house had been built, back in the 1840's, was now situated *inside* the house, in the middle of the hallway. It so happened this was the exact spot where the ghostly footsteps had always stopped dead.

The soft footsteps they took to be the sailor's were never heard again nor was anything happening that they could consciously connect with him. They assumed the phenomena he might have caused were merely his way of saying good-bye and that he had long since found a better place to hang around.

But the heavy footsteps, and the man in gray remained. So did the mystery of who he was and why he was disturbing the peace of the house. Judy started to talk to various neighbors and take frequent trips to the local library. Under the guise of doing research into the background of their house for reasons of historical curiosity, the girl managed to dredge up quite a bit of information, not necessarily all of it reliable or even true.

The trouble was that in the nineteenth century, Main Street had not yet been named, and the town was quite different. It was difficult to trace individual addresses. There was, for instance, the rumor that 80 years ago a grocer named Jack Meyer had been murdered in their house. She tried to get proof of this and found that a certain George Meyer, occupation unknown, had indeed been murdered in 1888 in Belleville, Illinois. But there was nothing to show that he had resided at this address.

She continued to search and finally hit paydirt. The local paper of Tuesday, June 26, 1923, carried a one-column notice that immediately excited her.

*Jacob Meyer, aged 77, shot himself today. Aged west side coal miner was despondent because of ill health. Was found dead in chair by wife, bullet through his brain.*

Apparently Meyer had been brooding over his bad health the night before. At 10:15 he had lunch — miners rise early for breakfast — and then took a rest in his usual chair. When his wife called out to him and got no reply, she checked to see what was the matter and found blood trickling down his face. Horrified, she called on her brother Alex White to come and help. The brother, who resided next door, came and found life ebbing from the aged man. An instant later, Meyer was dead. At his feet was the .32 caliber revolver he had used to blow his brains out. The bullet had passed through his head and lay nearby on the floor. What was strange that *nobody had heard the shot*, even though several members of the family had been within a few feet of the man all that time. How was it possible? Evidently he had held the gun to his temple and fired at close range and the sound had somehow been muffled.

There had been no threat of suicide beforehand, but Meyer had told his wife on arising, "Mary, I am feeling very bad today."

Meyer had retired six months before due to failing health. Prior to that he had still worked at a nearby mine despite his advanced age. A native of Germany, where he had been born in 1845, Meyer had come to America to seek his fortune.

Judy Walta put the clipping down and suddenly many things began to fall in place for her.

Why hadn't the ghost shown his face? Was he ashamed of having committed suicide, considered an act of cowardice in those days? Or was it because the bullet had literally torn his face to shreds?

The footsteps were those of a heavy man. Meyer was a heavy man. But the man in gray did not look 77 years of age. This at first threw the sisters for a loop until they understood, from psychic literature, that the dead usually return in their mental imagines to that which they consider the prime of life — usually around age thirty, or thereabouts.

They had noticed that the phenomena occurred toward the end of the month, usually after the twentieth and at no other times.

Meyer had killed himself June 26, 1923. The suicide, according to the newspaper, took place at their address, in their house, which was Meyer's at the time.

The sound, heard by Judy, of a package dropping sharply to the floor could very well have been a reenactment of the fatal shot that killed him.

In Jacob Meyer's day, the entrance was to the rear of the house and he would have come home that way, every day, from the mine. Was he simply continuing to go through his daily routine, refusing to accept the reality of his suicide?

Somehow the understanding of the problem changed the atmosphere in the house. Not that the phenomena ceased — far from it — but it appeared that the ghostly resident had finally found a kind of relationship with the flesh-and-blood inhabitants of what was once his home.

Cigar smoke now could be smelled on several occasions, although there was no cigar smoker in the house and all doors and windows were shut airtight. The smoke did not originate outside the house. This smell was soon followed or rather augmented by the smell of freshly brewed coffee at times when no one was brewing any coffee. The sound of papers rattling, someone sitting down in the chair as if to read his newspaper over his morning coffee and perhaps smoke a cigar, and scraping noises of a chair being half-dragged across the floor in plain view of the sisters contributed to their conviction that their ghostly visitor, far from being ready to leave upon being recognized, was getting read for a long — to him — comfortable stay.

If the young women had any doubts as to the identity of the unbidden guest, these were soon dispelled. On the night of April 27, 1967, Dollie and Judy were about to leave the studio for the night, when they both distinctly heard the sound of a shot coming from inside the building. They had just locked the back door and knew the house was quite empty. They debated whether to run or go back in and check. Curiosity won out, they unlocked the door again and went back inside. They checked the studio and nothing was out of place. They had just gotten ready to leave again, when they heard another shot. The second shot sounded quite *muffled*, whereas the first one had been loud and clear. It came from the area of the furnace room in the middle of the house.

In November, Dollie was walking under the doorway between the front and back rooms, an area hitherto free from psychic phenomena. She was stopped cold by something that resisted her advance although she could not see anything unusual. She felt that she was walking through heavy water, halfway up to her knees. This was a physical thing, she realized, and in sudden horror it occurred to her that she was trying to penetrate the etheric body of Mr. Meyer. Hastily retreating she left the house in a hurry.

That same month a hat disappeared without a trace. Judy had bought it for a friend for Christmas and had kept it in a box along with other Christmas gifts. None of the other items were disturbed, but the hat was gone. The puzzle was made worse by her discovery, several days later, of three dollar bills in the receipt book. Since neither of the girls nor anyone else had placed them there, this was strange indeed. On checking their receipts and figures, they found they were exactly three dollars over. It so happened that the hat, which was never seen again, had cost three dollars.

The reputation of the house as a haunted abode seeped out despite the sisters' reluctance to discuss it except, when necessary, with their friends and pupils. One day a woman walked by the house to see if she could have a look at the "ghost." As she looked at the front windows, she found herself tripped by an unseen force. Neighbors picked her up, but word got back to Judy and she interviewed the lady afterwards. Shaking her head, the woman insisted nothing had happened, she had not fallen. Judy was happy to let it go at that. Who wants to admit being tripped by the ghost of a man dead for forty years?

About the time, Judy discovered that the ghostly miner's wedding to Mary White had taken place on September 9, 1867. When a man celebrates his one hundredth wedding anniversary, he should not have time for such foolishness as tripping people outside haunted houses. Quite possibly Mrs. Meyer has since taken him in hand and made a better home for him beyond the veil. At any rate, the door in the rear no longer opens and closes as it used to, and perhaps Jacob Meyer is now retired for good.

# 8
# The Ghost of the California Sailor

One night in the early spring of 1965, the telephone rang and a pleasant voice said, "I think I've got a case for you, Mr. Holzer. I'm calling from Alameda, California."

Before the young lady could run up an impressive telephone bill, I stopped her and asked her to jot down the main points of her story for my records. She promised this, but took several months to comply. Evidently the ghost was not so unpleasant as she thought it was the night she had to call me long distance, or perhaps she had learned to live with the unseen visitor.

It had all started four years before when Gertrude Frost's grandmother bought a house in Alameda, an island in San Francisco Bay connected with the mainland by a causeway and mainly covered by small homes — many of which belong to people connected with the nearby naval installations. The house itself was built around 1917.

After the old woman died, Miss Frost's mother had the house. Noises in the night when no one was about kept Miss Frost and her mother and aunt from ever getting a good night's sleep. It did not sound like a very exciting case and I was frankly skeptical since there are many instances where people *think* they hear unnatural noises when in fact they merely ascribe super-normal character to what is actually natural in origin. But I was going to be in the area, and decided to drop in.

I asked Claude Mann, a news reporter from Oakland's Channel 2, to accompany us — my wife Catherine and my good friend Sybil Leek, who did not have the faintest idea where Alameda was or that we were going there. Not that Sybil cared — it was merely another assignment and she was willing. The date was July 1, 1965, and it was pleasantly warm — in fact, a most unghostly type of day.

As soon as we approached the little house, we unloaded the camera equipment and went inside where two of the ladies were expecting us. I promptly put Sybil into one of the easy chairs and began my work — or rather Sybil began hers.

Although the house was in the middle of the island and no indication of the ocean could be seen anywhere near it, Sybil at once remarked that she felt the sea was connected with the house in some way; she felt a presence in the house but not associated with it directly.

As soon as Sybil was in deep trance, someone took over her vocal cords.

"What is your name?" I asked.

"Dominic . . ."

"Do you live in this house?"

"No house . . . water . . . fort . . . tower . . ."

"What are you doing here?"

"Have to wait . . . Triana . . ."

"What does Triana mean?"

"*Triana* . . . boat. . . ."

"Where does the boat go?"

"Hokeite . . . Hokeite . . ."

"What year is this?"

"1902."

"What is your rank?"

"Mid-ship-man." He had difficulty in enunciating. The voice had a strangely unreal quality, not at all like Sybil's normal speaking voice but more like the thin voice of a young man.

I continued to question the ghostly visitor.

"Are you serving on this boat?"

"Left here," he replied. "I'm going to break . . . everything up."

"Why do you want to do that?"

"Those things . . . got to go . . . because they're untidy . . . I shall break them up . . . they say I'm mad . . . I'm not mad . . ."

"How old are you?"

"Thirty-one . . ."

"Where were you born?"

"I was born . . . Hakeipe. . . ."

I was not sure whether he said "Hakeipe" or "Hakeite," but it sounded something like that.

"What state?" I had never heard of such a place.

"No state," the ghost said, somewhat indignant because I did not know better.

"Then where is it?" I demanded.

"In Japan," the ghost informed me. I began to wonder if he didn't mean Hakodate, a harbor of some importance. It had a fair number of foreign people at all times, being one of the principal seaports for the trade with America and Europe. It would be pronounced "Hak-o-deit," not too different from what I had heard through Sybil's mediumship.

"Break them up, break them up," the ghost continued to mumble menacingly, "throw those little things . . . into . . . faces . . . I don't like faces . . . people . . ."

"Do you realize time has gone on?"

"Time goes on," the voice said sadly.

"What are you doing here?" I asked.

"What are *they* doing here?" the ghost shot back angrily.

It was his land, he asserted. I asked if he had built anything on it.

"The tower is here," he said cryptically, "to watch the ships. I stay here."

"Are you American?"

"No, I'm Italian."

"Are you a merchant sailor or Navy?"

"Navy . . . why don't you go away?"

"What do you want here?"

"Nothing . . ."

I explained about his death and this evoked cold anger.

"Smash everything . . ."

I decided to change the subject before the

snarling became completely unintelligible.

Meanwhile, Claude Mann's cameras were busily humming.

"Did you serve in the American Navy?"

"Yes."

"Give me your serial number!"

"Serial . . . one . . . eight . . . eight . . . four . . . three."

"Where did you enlist?"

"Hakkaite."

It did not make sense to me, so I repeated the question. This time the answer was different. Perhaps he had not understood the first time.

"In 'meda," he said.

Sailors call Alameda by this abbreviation. How could Sybil, newly arrived here, have known this? She could not, and I did not.

"Who's your commanding officer?"

"Oswald Gregory."

"What rank?"

"Captain."

"The name of your ship."

"*Triana*."

"How large a ship?"

"I don't know. . . ."

I asked about his family. Did he have a wife? Was he well? He became more and more reluctant. Finally he said: "I'm not answering questions... . ."

"Your father's name?" I continued.

"Guiseppe."

"Mother?"

"Matilone. . . ."

"Sister or brothers?"

"Four. . . ."

They live in "Hokkeipe," he added.

"Where did you go to school?"

"Hokkeipe Mission. . . ."

He came to this place in 1902, he asserted, and was left behind because he was sick.

"I wait for next trip . . . but they never came back. I had bad headache. I was lying here. Not a house. Water."

I then asked what he was doing to let people know about his presence.

"I can walk — as well as anyone," he boasted. "I play with water, I drop things. . . ."

I reasoned with him. His father and mother were waiting for him. Didn't he want to be with them? I received a flat, "No." He wasn't interested in a family reunion. I tried to explain about real estate. I explained that the house was fully paid for and he was trespassing. He could not have cared less.

I questioned his honesty and he did not like that. It made him waver in his determination to break everything up.

I spoke to him of the "other side" of life. He asked that I take him there.

He now recalled his sisters' names, Matild' and Alissi, or something that sounded like it.

"We've come to fetch you, Dominic," I said, suggesting he "go across."

"You're late," he snarled.

"Better late than never," I intoned.

"I was never late," he complained. "I can walk . . . without you!"

Gratitude was not his forte.

I requested that Sybil return to her own body now, but to remain in trance so as to answer my questions on what she could observe in that state.

Soon Sybil's own voice, feeble at first, was heard again from her lips.

I asked her to describe the scene she saw.

"I see a short, dark man," she replied, "who can't walk very well; he was insane. I think he had fits. Fell down. Violent man."

"Do you see a house?"

"No, I see water, and a gray ship. Big ship, not for people. Not for traveling. Low ship."

"Do you see a name on the ship?"

" . . . *Ana* . . . can't see it properly."

"What is this man doing here?"

"He had a fit here, and fell down and died, and somebody left him here. Somebody picked the body up . . . into the water . . ."

Sybil showed signs of strain and I decided to take her out of trance. As soon as she was "back" to her own self — not remembering anything, of course, that had come through her the past hour — I turned to Miss Frost to find out what it was exactly that had occurred here of an unusual nature.

"Always this uneasy feeling . . . causing nervousness . . . more at night . . ." she explained, "and noises like small firecrackers."

Miss Frost is a woman in her thirties, pleasant

and soft-spoken, and she holds a responsible position in San Francisco business life.

"If you pay no attention to it," she added, "then it becomes more intense, louder."

"Doesn't want to be ignored, eh?" I said.

"Occasionally at night you hear footsteps in the living room."

"When it is empty?"

"Of course."

"What does it sound like?"

"As if there were no carpets . . . like walking on boards . . . a man's footsteps."

"How often?"

"Maybe three times . . . last time was about three months ago. We've been here four years, but we only heard it about half a year after we moved in. Once there was a noise inside the buffet as if there were a motor in it, which of course there isn't."

"Has anyone else had any experiences of an unusual nature in this house?"

"A painter who was painting a small room in the rear of the house suddenly asked me for water because he didn't feel well. Because of the noises."

I turned to Miss Frost's aunt, who had sat by quietly, listening to our conversation.

"Have you heard these footsteps?"

"Yes," she said. "I checked up and there was nobody there who could have caused them. That was around two in the morning. Sometimes around five or six also. They went around the bed. We had the light on, but it continued."

With the help of Miss Frost, I was able to trace

the history of the area. Before the house was built here, the ground was part of the Cohen estate. The water is not far from the house although one cannot actually see it from the house.

Originally Alameda was inhabited by Indians and much of it was used as burial ground. Even today bones are dug up now and again.

Prior to Miss Frost, a Mr. Bequette owned the house, but what interested me far more than Mr. Bequette was the fact that many years ago a hospital occupied the land at this spot.

In 1941, allegedly, a family lived at this house whose son was killed in action during the war. A mysterious letter reached Miss Frost in February of 1961 addressed to a B. Biehm at her address, but she could not locate this person.

None of this takes us back to 1902 when Dominic said he lived. A Japanese-born Italian sailor serving in the U.S. Navy is a pretty unusual combination. Was Dominic his family name?

I decided to query the Navy Department in the hope that they might have some records about such a man, although I had learned on previous occasions that Naval records that far back are not always complete.

On December 29th, 1966, I received this reply from the office of the Chief of Naval Operations:

> Dear Mr. Holzer:
>
> In reply to your letter of 8 December, we have been unable to find either DOMINIC or Oswald GREGORY in the lists of U.S. Navy

officers during this century. The Navy Registers for the period around 1902 list no U.S. Naval ship named TRIANA.

We have very little information on Alameda Island during the early 1900's. The attached extract from the Naval Air Station history, however, may be of some use.

Sincerely yours,
F. KENT LOOMIS
Captain, USN (Ret.)
Asst. Director of
Naval History

Captain Loomis enclosed a history of the Alameda installations which seems to confirm the picture painted of the area (prior to that installation) by the ghostly sailor.

The real story of the U.S. Naval Air Station, Alameda, is how it has "arisen from the waters." How it was thrown up from the bottom of San Francisco Bay; how it was anchored to the earth with grass roots; how it was, by accident, the scene of some of the earliest flights in America. This is the romance of Alameda.

The Navy Department first began to consider the site now occupied by the air station toward the end of the First World War. The intention was to utilize the site as a destroyer base, but the war was over before the plans could be perfected. The land then lapsed into oblivion. *It was a rather barren land.* When the tide was out it was odious and disagreeable looking. Since people who boil soap are not fastidious concerning olfactory matters, the Twenty Mule Team Borax Company located the site of their first efforts near the "Mole," which went to San Francisco's ferries.

The main part of Alameda was very pretty, covered with good rich "bottom land" and shade trees, from which it had derived its name during the Spanish occupation days. "Alameda" means "shade" or "shady lane."

In 1776, the land had been granted to Don Luis Peralta, a grizzled old man who immigrated from Tabac in Sonora. His life as a soldier had been crowded with 40 years of service to His Majesty, the King of Spain, and ten children. It was only a small part of the 43,000 acres granted him by a grateful Spain.

He distributed his lands among his children when he felt his time had come. Although the peninsula of Alameda was in the most part fertile, the western tip of it was nothing but barren sands and tidal flats.

In 1876, engineers cut a channel through the peninsula's tip which linked San Leandro Bay with the main bay, and Alameda became an island. Deep water was on the way, and dredging was begun to effect this end.

The inability of the U.S. Navy librarian to identify a ship named the *Triana* did not stop me from looking further. Was there ever such a ship? A Captain Treeana commanded one of the ships of Christopher Columbus, and consequently there are towns named for him in the land he and his shipmates helped discover. Spelled nowadays Triana, one is in Alabama, and in the city of Huntsville there is a Triana Boulevard. It seems highly likely that so famous a captain's name should at one time or other have been chosen as the name of a ship.

Meanwhile, back at the house, things remained quiet and peaceful for 48 hours. Miss Frost was happy for the first time in years.

And then the footsteps and other noises resumed. Dominic wasn't going to ship out, after all.

That was in July 1965. I made certain suggestions. Close the door mentally; gently tell the ghost he must go, over and over again. He was free now to do so — proof of which was the fact that his footsteps, once confined to the living room area, were now heard all over the house.

A year has gone by, and I have had no news from Alameda. Perhaps no news is good news and the ghostly sailor roams no more.

# 9
# The Ghost on the Porch

Mrs. Ethel Meyers, who has frequently accompanied me on ghost-hunting expeditions, heard from friends living in Bergen County, New Jersey, about some unusual happenings at their very old house.

Eventually, the "safari for ghost" was organized, and Mr. B., the master of the house, picked us up in his car and drove us to Bergen County. The house turned out to be a beautifully preserved pre-Revolutionary house set within an enclosure of lawn and tall trees.

The building had been started in 1704, I later learned, and the oldest portion was the right wing; the central portion was added in the latter part of the eighteenth century, and the final, frontal portion was built from old materials about fifty years ago, carefully preserving the original style of the house. The present owners had acquired it about a year ago from a family who had been in possession for several generations. The house was then empty, and the B.'s refurbished it completely in excellent taste with antiques of the period.

After they moved into the house, they slept for a few days on a mattress on the enclosed porch, which skirted the west wing of the house. Their furniture had not yet arrived, and they didn't mind roughing it for a short while. It was summer, and not too cool.

In the middle of the night, Mrs. B. suddenly awoke with the uncanny feeling that there was *someone else* in the house, besides her husband and herself. She got up and walked toward the corridor-like extension of the enclosed porch running along the back of the house. There she clearly distinguished the figure of a man, seemingly white, with a beard, wearing what she described as "something ruffly white." She had the odd sensation that this man belonged to a much earlier period than the present. The light was good enough to see the man clearly for about five minutes, in which she was torn between fear of the intruder and curiosity. Finally, she approached him, and saw him *literally dissolve before her very eyes!* At the same time, she had the odd sensation that the stranger came to look *them* over, wondering what they were doing in *his* house! Mrs. B., a celebrated actress and choreographer, is not a scoffer, nor is she easily susceptible. Ghosts to her are something one can discuss intelligently. Since her husband shared this view, they inquired of the former owner about any possible hauntings.

"I've never heard of any or seen any," Mr. S. told them, "but my daughter-in-law has never been able to sleep in the oldest part of the house. Said there was too much going on there. Also, one of the neighbors claims he saw *something*."

Mr. S. wasn't going to endanger his recent real-estate transaction with too many ghostly tales. The B.'s thanked him and settled down to life in their colonial house.

But they soon learned that theirs was a busy place indeed. Both are artistic and very intuitive, and they soon became aware of the presence of unseen forces.

One night Mrs. B. was alone at home, spending the evening in the upper story of the house. There was nobody downstairs. Suddenly she heard the downstairs front door open and shut. There was no mistaking the very characteristic and complex sound of the opening of this ancient lock! Next, she heard footsteps, and sighed with relief. Apparently her husband had returned much earlier than expected. Quickly, she rushed down the stairs to welcome him. There was nobody there. There was no one in front of the door. All she found was the cat in a strangely excited state!

Sometime after, Mr. B. came home. For his wife these were anxious hours of waiting. He calmed her as best he could, having reservations about the whole incident. Soon these doubts were to be dispelled completely.

This time Mrs. B. was away and Mr. B. was alone in the downstairs part of the house. The maid was asleep in her room, the B.'s child fast asleep upstairs. It was a peaceful evening, and Mr. B. decided to have a snack. He found himself in the kitchen, which is located at the western end of the downstairs part of the house, *when he suddenly heard a car drive up*. Next, there were the distinct sounds of the front door opening and closing again. As he rushed to the front door, he heard the dog bark furiously. But again, there was no one either inside or outside the house!

Mr. B., a star and director, and as rational a man as could be, wondered if he had imagined these things. But he knew he had not. What he had heard were clearly the noises of an arrival. While he was still trying to sort out the meaning of all this, another strange thing happened.

A few evenings later, he found himself alone in the downstairs living room, when he heard carriage wheels outside grind to a halt. He turned his head toward the door, wondering who it might be at this hour. The light was subdued, but good enough to read by. He didn't have to wait long. A short, husky man walked into the room *through* the closed door; then, without paying attention to Mr. B., turned and walked out into the oldest part of the house, again *through a closed door!*

"What did he look like to you?" I asked.

"He seemed dotted, as if he were made of thick, solid dots, and he wore a long coat, the kind they used to wear around 1800. He probably was the same man my wife encountered."

"You think he is connected with the oldest part of the house?"

"Yes, I think so. About a year ago I played some

very old lute music, the kind popular in the eighteenth century, in there — and something happened to the atmosphere in the room. As if someone were listening quietly and peacefully."

But it wasn't always as peaceful in there. A day before our arrival, Mrs. B. had lain down, trying to relax. But she could not stay in the old room. "There was someone there," she said simply.

The B.'s weren't the only ones to hear and see ghosts. Last summer, two friends of the B.'s were visiting them, and everybody was seated in the living room, when in plain view of all the screen door to the porch opened and closed again *by its own volition!* Needless to add, the friends didn't stay long.

Only a day before our visit, another friend had tried to use the small washroom in the oldest part of the house. Suddenly, he felt chills coming on and rushed out of the room, telling Mrs. B. that "someone was looking at him."

At this point, dinner was ready, and a most delicious repast it was. Afterwards we accompanied the B.'s into the oldest part of their house, a low-ceilinged room dating back to the year 1704. Two candles provided the only light, Mrs. Meyers got into a comfortable chair, and gradually drifted into a trance.

"Marie . . . Catherine . . . who calls?" she mumbled.

"Who is it?" I inquired.

"Pop . . . live peacefully . . . love. . . ."

"What is your name?" I wanted to know.

"Achabrunn. . . ."

I didn't realize it at the time, but a German family named Achenbach had built the house and owned it for several generations. Much later still, I found out that one of the children of the builder had been called Marian.

I continued my interrogation.

"Who rules this country?"

"The Anglish. George."

"What year is this?"

"Fifty-six. Seventeen fifty six."

"When did you stay here?"

"Always. Pop. My house. *You* stay with *me.*"

Then the ghost spoke haltingly of his family, his children, of which he had nine, three of whom had gone away.

"What can we do for you?" I said, hoping to find the reason for the many disturbances.

"Yonder over side hill, hillock, three buried . . . flowers there."

"Do you mean," I said, "that we should put flowers on these graves?"

The medium seemed excited.

"*Ach Gott, ja, machs gut.*" With this the medium crossed herself.

"What is your name?" I asked again.

"Oterich . . . Oblich . . ." The medium seemed hesitant as if the ghost were searching his memory for his own name. Later, I found that the name given was pretty close to that of another family having a homestead next door.

The ghost continued.

"She lady . . . I not good. I very stout heart, I look up to good-blood lady, I make her good . . . Kathrish, holy lady, I worship lady . . . they rest on hill too, with three. . . ."

After the seance, I found a book entitled *Pre-Revolutionary Dutch Houses in Northern New Jersey and New York.* It was here that I discovered the tradition that a poor shepherd from Saxony married a woman above his station, and built this very house. The year 1756 was correct.

But back to my interrogation. "Why don't you rest on the hillock?"

"I take care of . . . four . . . hillock . . . Petrish. Ladian, Annia, Kathrish. . . ."

Then, as if taking cognizance of us, he added — "To care for you, that's all I want."

Mrs. B. nodded and said softly, "You're always welcome here."

Afterward, I found that there were indeed some graves on the hill beyond the house.

From Mr. B. I learned that underground passages are known to exist between this house and the so-called Slave House, across the road.

The ghost then revealed that his wife's father, an Englishman, had built the passage, and that stores were kept in it.

"Where were you born?" I inquired.

"Here. Bergenville."

Bergenville proved to be the old name of the township.

I then delicately told him that this was 1960. He seemed puzzled, to say the least.

"In 1756 I was sixty-five years old. I am not 204 years older?"

At this point, the ghost recognized the women's clothing the medium was wearing, and tore at them. I explained how we were able to "talk" to him. He seemed pacified.

"You'll accept my maize, my wine, my whiskey. . . ."

I discovered that maize and wine staples were the mainstays of the area at that period.

Suddenly the ghost withdrew and after a moment another person, a woman, took over the medium. Then she too withdrew, and Mrs. Meyers returned to her own body, none the worse for her experiences, none of which, incidentally, she remembered.

Shortly afterward, we returned to New York. It was as if we had just come from another world. Leaving the poplar-lined road behind us, we gradually re-entered the world of gasoline and dirt that is the modern city.

Nothing further has been reported from the house in Bergen County, but I am sure the ghost, whom Mrs. B. had asked to stay as long as he wished, is still there. There is of course now no further need to bang doors, to call attention to his lonely self. *They know he is there with them.*

# 10
# A Ghost in Maine

Port Clyde is a lovely little fishing village on the coast of Maine where a small number of native Yankees try to cope with a few summer residents, usually from New York or the Midwest. Their worlds do not really mesh, but the old-timers realize that a little — not too much — tourism is really quite good for business, especially the few small hotels in and around Port Clyde and St. George, so they don't mind them too much. But the Down Easterners do keep to themselves, and it isn't always easy to get them to open up about their private lives or such things as, let us say, ghosts.

Carol Olivieri Schulte lived in Council Bluffs, Iowa, when she first contacted me in November 1974. The wife of a lawyer, she is an inquisitive lady, a college graduate, and the mother of what was then a young son. Somehow Carol had gotten hold of some of my books and become intrigued by them, especially where ghosts were concerned, because she, too, had had a brush with the uncanny.

"It was the summer of 1972," she explained to me, "and I was sleeping in an upstairs bedroom," in the summer cottage her parents owned in Port Clyde, Maine.

"My girlfriend Marion and her boyfriend were across the hall with their animals, a Siamese cat and two dogs."

The cat had been restless and crept into Carol's room, touching her pillow and waking her. Carol sat up in bed ready to turn on the light, when she saw standing beside her bed a female figure in a very white nightgown. The figure had small shoulders and long, flowing hair . . . and Carol could see right through her!

It became apparent, as she came closer, that she wanted to get Carol's attention, trying to talk with her hands.

"Her whole body suggested she was in desperate need of something. Her fingers were slender, and there was a diamond ring on her fourth finger, on the right hand. Her hands moved more desperately as I ducked under the covers."

Shortly after this, Carol had a dream contact with the same entity. This time she was in another room in the house, sleeping, when she saw the same young woman. She appeared to her at first in the air, smaller than life size. With her was a small child, a boy of perhaps three years of age, also dressed in a white gown. While the child was with Carol on her bed, in the dream, the mother hovered at some distance in the corner. Carol, in the dream, had the feeling the mother had turned the child over to her, as if to protect him, and then she vanished. Immediately there followed the appearance of another woman, a black-hooded female, seeming very old, coming toward her and the child. Carol began to realize the dark-hooded woman wanted to take the child from her, and the child was afraid and clung to her. When the woman stood close to Carol's bed, still in the dream, Carol noticed her bright green eyes and crooked, large nose, and her dark complexion. She decided to fight her off, concentrating her thoughts on the white light she knew was an expression of psychic protection, and the dark-hooded woman disappeared. Carol was left with the impression that she had been connected with a school or institution of some kind. At this, the mother in her white nightgown returned and took the child back, looking at Carol with an expression of gratitude before disappearing again along with her child.

Carol woke up, but the dream was so vivid it stayed with her for weeks. Even when she contacted me, it was still crystal clear in her mind. One more curious event transpired at the exact time Carol had overcome the evil figure in the dream. Her grandmother, whom she described as "a very reasoning, no-nonsense lively Yankee lady," had a cottage right in back of Carol's parents'. She was tending her stove, as she had done many times before, when it blew up right into her face. There was nothing whatever wrong with the stove.

Carol had had psychic experiences before, and

even her attorney husband was familiar with the world of spirits, so her contacting me for help was by no means a family problem.

I was delighted to hear from her, not because a Maine ghost was so very different from the many other ghosts I had dealt with through the years, but because of the timing of Carol's request. It so happened that at that time I was in the middle of writing, producing, and appearing in the NBC series *In Search of . . .*, and the ghost house in Maine would make a fine segment.

An agreement was arranged among all concerned — Carol, her husband, her parents, the broadcasting management, and me. I then set about to arrange a schedule for our visit. We had to fly into Rockland, Maine, and then drive down to Port Clyde. If I wanted to do it before Carol and her family were in residence, that, too, would be all right though she warned me about the cold climate up there during the winter months.

In the end we decided on May, when the weather would be acceptable, and the water in the house would be turned back on.

I had requested that all witnesses of actual phenomena in the house be present to be questioned by me.

Carol then sent along pictures of the house and statements from some of the witnesses. I made arrangements to have her join us at the house for the investigation and filming for the period of May 13 to 15, 1976. The team — the crew, my psychic, and me — would all stay over at a local hotel. The psychic was a young woman artist named Ingrid Beckman with whom I had been working and helping develop her gift.

And so it happened that we congregated at Port Clyde from different directions, but with one purpose in mind — to contact the lady ghost at the house. As soon as we had settled in at the local hotel, the New Ocean House, we drove over to the spanking-white cottage that was to be the center of our efforts for the next three days. Carol's brother Robert had driven up from Providence, and her close friend Marion Going from her home, also in Rhode Island.

I asked Ingrid to stay at a little distance from the house and wait for me to bring her inside, while I spoke to some of the witnesses out of Ingrid's earshot. Ingrid understood and sat down on the lawn, taking in the beauty of the landscape.

Carol and I walked in the opposite direction, and once again we went over her experiences as she had reported them to me in her earlier statement. But was there anything beyond that, I wondered, and questioned Carol about it. "Now since that encounter with the ghostly lady have you seen her again? Have you ever heard her again?"

"Well about three weeks ago before I was to come out here, I really wanted to communicate with her. I concentrated on it just before I went to sleep, you know. I was thinking about it, and I dreamed that she appeared to me the way she had in the dream that followed her apparition here in this house. And then I either dreamed that I woke up momentarily and saw her right there as I had actually seen her in this bedroom or I actually did wake up and see her. Now the sphere of consciousness I was in — I am doubtful as to where I was at that point. I mean it was nothing like the experience I experienced right here in this room. I was definitely awake, and *I definitely saw that ghost.* As to this other thing a couple of weeks ago — I wasn't quite sure."

"Was there any kind of message?"

"No, not this last time."

"Do you feel she was satisfied having made contact with you?"

"Yeah, I felt that she wanted to communicate with me in the same sense that I wanted to communicate with her. Like an old friend will want to get in touch with another old friend, and I get the feeling she was just saying, 'Yes, I'm still here.' "

I then turned to Carol's brother, Bob Olivieri, and questioned him about his own encounters with anything unusual in the house. He took me to the room he was occupying at the time of the experiences, years ago, but apparently the scene was still very fresh in his mind.

"Mr. Olivieri, what exactly happened to you in this room?"

"Well, one night I was sleeping on this bed and all of a sudden I woke up and heard footsteps — what I thought were footsteps — it sounded like slippers or baby's feet in pajamas — something like that. Well, I woke up and I came over, and I stepped in this spot, and I looked in the hallway and the sound stopped. I thought maybe I was imagining it. So I came back to the bed, got into bed again, and again I heard footsteps. Well, this time I got up and as soon as I came to the same spot again and looked into the hallway it stopped. I figured it was my nephew. So I walked down the hallway and looked into the room where my sister and nephew were, and they were both sound asleep. I checked my parents' room, and they were also asleep. I just walked back.

"I didn't know what to do so I got into bed again, and I kept on hearing them. I kept on walking over, and they would still be going until I stepped in this spot where they would stop. As soon as I stepped here. And this happened for an hour. I kept getting up. Heard the footsteps, stepped in this spot, and they stopped. So finally I got tired of it and came over to my bed and lay down in bed and as soon as I lay down I heard the steps again, exactly what happened before — and they seemed to stop at the end of the hallway. A few minutes later I felt a pressure on my sheets, starting from my feet, and going up, up, up, going up further, further, slowly but surely . . . and finally something pulled my hair! Naturally I was just scared for the rest of the night. I couldn't get to sleep."

I thought it was time to get back to Ingrid and bring her into the house. This I did, with the camera people following us every step of the way to record for NBC what might transpire. Just before we entered the house, Ingrid turned to me and said, "You know that window up there? When we first arrived, I noticed someone standing in it."

"What exactly did you see?"

"It was a woman . . . and she was looking out at us."

The house turned out to be a veritable jewel of Yankee authenticity, the kind of house a sea captain might be happy in, or perhaps only a modern antiquarian. The white exterior was matched by a spanking-clean, sometimes-sparse interior, with every piece of furniture of the right period — nineteenth and early twentieth centuries — and a feeling of being lived in by many people, for many years.

After we had entered the downstairs part where there was an ample kitchen and a nice day room, I asked Ingrid, as usual, to tell me whatever psychic impression she was gathering about the house, its people, and its history. Naturally, I had made sure all along that Ingrid knew nothing of the house or the quest we had come on to Maine, and there was absolutely no way she could have had access to specifics about the area, the people in the house — past and present — nor anything at all about the case.

Immediately Ingrid set to work. She seemed agitated.

"There is a story connected here with the eighteen twenties or the eighteen fourties," she began, and I turned on my tape recorder to catch the impressions she received as we went along. At first, they were conscious psychic readings; later, Ingrid seemed in a slight state of trance and communication with spirit entities directly. Here is what followed.

"Eighteen twenties and eighteen forties. Do you mean both, or one or the other?"

"Well, it's in that time period. And I sense a woman with a great sense of remorse."

"Do you feel this is a presence here?"

"Definitely a presence here."

"What part of the house do you feel it's strongest in?"

"Well, I'm being told to go upstairs."

"Is a force pulling you up?"

"No, I just have a feeling to go upstairs."

"Before you go upstairs, before you came here did you have any feeling that there was something to it?"

"Yes, several weeks ago I saw a house — actually it was a much older house than this one, and it was on this site — and it was a dark house and it was shingled and it was — as I say, could have been an eighteenth-century house, the house that I saw. It looked almost like a salt box, it had that particular look. And I saw that it was right on the water and I sensed a woman in it and a story concerned with a man in the sea with this house."

"A man with the sea?"

"Yes."

"Do you feel that this entity is still in the house?"

"I do, and of course I don't feel this is the *original* house. I feel it was on this property, and this is why I sense that she is throughout the house. That she comes here because this is her re-enactment."

I asked her to continue.

"I can see in my mind's eye the house that was on this property before, and in my mind I sense a field back in this direction, and there was land that went with this!"

"Now we are upstairs. I want you to look into every room and give me your impressions of it," I said.

"Well, the upstairs is the most active. I sense a woman who is waiting. This is in the same time period. There are several other periods that go with this house, but I will continue with this one. I also see that she has looked out — not from this very same window, but windows in this direction of the house — *waiting for somebody to come back.*"

"What about this room?"

"Well, this room is like the room where she conducted a vigil, waiting for someone. And I just got an impression where she said that, 'She' meaning a schooner, 'was built on the Kennebec River.' . . . It seems to be a double-masted schooner, and it seems to be her husband who is on this. And I have an impression of novelties that he has brought her back. Could be from a foreign country. Perhaps the Orient or something like that."

"Now go to the corridor again and try some of the other rooms. What about this one?"

"I sense a young man in this room, but this is from a different time period. It's a young boy. It seems to be the nineteen twenties."

"Is that all you sense in this room?"

"That is basically what I sense in this room. The woman of the double-masted schooner story is throughout the house because as I have said, she doesn't really belong to this house. She is basically on the *property* — mainly she still goes through this whole house looking for the man to come home. And the front of the house is where the major activity is. She is always watching. But I have an impression now of a storm that she is very upset about. A gale of some kind. It seems to be November. I also feel she is saying something about . . . flocking sheep. There are sheep on this property."

"Where would you think is the most active room?"

"The most active room I think is upstairs and to the front, where we just were. I feel it most strongly there."

"Do you think we might be able to make contact with her?"

"Yes, I think so. Definitely I feel that she is watching *and I knew about her before I came.*"

"What does she look like?"

"I see a tall woman, who is rather thin and frail with dark hair and it appears to be a white gown. It could be a nightgown I see her in — it looks like a nightgown to me with a little embroidery on the front. Hand done."

"Let us see if she cares to make contact with us?"

"All right."

"If the entity is present, and wishes to talk to us, we have come as friends; she is welcome to use this instrument, Ingrid, to manifest."

"She is very unhappy here, Hans. She says her family hailed from England. I get her name as Margaret."

"Margaret what?"

"Something like Hogen — it begins with an H. I don't think it is Hogan. Hayden, or something like that. I'm not getting the whole name."

"What period are you in now?"

"Now she says eighteen forty-three. She is very unhappy because she wanted to settle in Kennebunk; she does not like it here. She doesn't like the responsibilities of the house. Her husband liked it in this fishing village. She is very unhappy about his choice."

"Is he from England?"

"Yes, their descendants are from England."

"You mean were they born here or in England?"

"That I'm not clear on. But they have told me that their descendants are English."

"Now is she here . . . ?"

"She calls Kennebunk the city. That to her is a center."

"What does she want? Why is she still here?"

"She's left with all this responsibility. Her husband went on a ship, to come back in two years."

"Did he?"

"No, she's still waiting for him."

"The name of the ship?"

"I think it's St. Catherine."

"Is it his ship? Is he a captain?"

"He is second in command. It's not a mate, but a second something or other."

"What is she looking for?"

"She's looking to be relieved."

"Of what?"

"Of the duties and the responsibilities."

"For what?"

"This house."

"Is she aware of her passing?"

"No, she's very concerned over the flocks. She says it's now come April, and it's time for shearing. She is very unhappy over this. In this direction, Hans, I can see what appears to be a barn, and it's very old-fashioned. She had two cows."

"Is she aware of the people in the house now?"

"She wants to communicate."

"What does she want them to do for her?"

"She wants for them to help her with the farm. She says it's too much, and the soil is all rocky and she can't get labor from the town. She's having a terrible time. It's too sandy here."

"Are there any children? Is she alone?"

"They have gone off, she says."

"And she's alone now?"

"Yes, she is."

"Can you see her?"

"Yes, I do see her."

"Can she see you?"

"Yes."

"Tell her that this is 1976, and that much time has passed. Does she understand this?"

"She just keeps complaining; she has nobody to write letters to."

"Does she understand that her husband has

passed on and that she herself is a spirit and that there is no need to stay if she doesn't wish to?"

"She needs to get some women from the town to help with the spinning."

"Tell her that the new people in the house are taking care of everything, and she is relieved and may go on. She's free to go."

"She said, 'to Kennebunk?' "

"Any place she wishes — to the city or to join her husband on the other side of life."

"She said, 'Oh, what I would do for a town house.' "

"Ask her to call out to her husband to take her away. He's waiting for her."

"What does Johnsbury mean? A Johnsbury."

"It's a place."

"She asking about Johnsbury."

"Does she wish to go there?"

"She feels someone may be there who could help her."

"Who?"

"It seems to be an uncle in Johnsbury."

"Then tell her to call out to her uncle in Johnsbury."

"She says he has not answered her letters."

"But if she speaks up now he will come for her. Tell her to do it now. Tell Margaret we are sending her to her uncle, with our love and compassion. That she need not stay here any longer. That she need not wait any longer for someone who cannot return. That she must go on to the greater world that awaits her outside, where she will rejoin her husband and she can see her uncle."

"She is wanting to turn on the lights. She is talking about the oil lamps. She wants them all lit."

"Tell her the people here will take good care of the house, of the lamps, and of the land."

"And she is saying, no tallow for the kitchen."

"Tell her not to worry."

"And the root cellar is empty."

"Tell her not to worry. We will take care of that for her. She is free to go — she is being awaited, she is being expected. Tell her to go on and go on from here in peace and with our love and compassion."

"She is looking for a lighthouse, or something about a lighthouse that disturbs her."

"What is the lighthouse?"

"She is very upset. She doesn't feel that it's been well kept; that this is one of the problems in this area. No one to tend things. 'I ought to be in Kennebunk,' she says, 'where it is a city.' "

"Who lives in Kennebunk that she knows?"

"No one she knows. She wants to go there."

"What will she do there?"

"Have a town house."

"Very well, then let her go to Kennebunk."

" 'And go [to] the grocer,' she says."

"Tell her she's free to go to Kennebunk. That we will send her there if she wishes. Does she wish to go to Kennebunk?"

"Yes, she does."

"Then tell her — tell her we are sending her now. With all our love . . ."

"In a carriage?"

"In a carriage."

"A black carriage with two horses."

"Very well. Is she ready to go?"

"Oh, I see her now in a fancy dress with a bonnet. But she's looking younger — she's looking much younger now. And I see a carriage out front with two dark horses and a man with a hat ready to take her."

"Did she get married in Kennebunk?"

"No."

"Where did she get married?"

"I don't get that."

"Is she ready to go?"

"Yes, she is."

"Tell her to get into the carriage and drive off."

"Yes, she's ready."

"Then go, Margaret — go."

"She says, many miles — three-day trip."

"All right. Go with our blessings. Do you see her in the carriage now?"

"Yes, the road goes this way. She is going down a winding road."

"Is she alone in the carriage?"

"Yes, she is, but there is a man driving."

"Who is the man who is driving?"

"A hired man."

"Is she in the carriage now?"

"Yes, she is."

"Is she on her way?"

"Yes."

"All right, then wave at her and tell her we send her away with our love."

"She looks to be about twenty-two now. Much younger."

"She's not to return to this house."

"She doesn't want to. She grew old in this house, she says."

"What was the house called then?"

"It was Point something."

"Did they build the house? She and her husband?"

"No, it was there."

"Who built it?"

"Samuel."

"And who was Samuel?"

"A farmer."

"They bought it from him?"

"Yes, they did. She says the deed is in the town hall."

"Of which town? Is it in this village?"

"Next town. Down the road."

"I understand. And in whose name is the deed?"

"Her husband's."

"First name."

"James."

"James what. Full name."

"It's something like Haydon."

"James Haydon from . . . ? What is Samuel's first name?"

"Samuels was the last name of the people who owned it."

"But the first name of the man who sold it. Does she remember that?"

"She never knew it."

"In what year was that?"

"Eighteen twenty-one."

"How much did they pay for the house?"

"Barter."

"What did they give them?"

"A sailing ship. A small sailing ship for fishing, and several horses. A year's supply of roots, and some paper — currency. Notes."

"But no money?"

"Just notes. Like promises, she says. Notes of promises."

"What was the full price of the house?"

"All in barter, all in exchange up here."

"But there was no sum mentioned for the house? No value?"

"She says, 'Ask my husband.' "

"Now did she and her husband live here alone?"

"Two children."

"What were their names?"

"Philip. But he went to sea."

"And the other one?"

"Francis."

"Did he go to sea too?"

"No."

"What happened to him?"

"I think Francis died."

"What did he die of?"

"Cholera. He was seventeen."

"Where did they get married? In what church?"

"Lutheran."

"Why Lutheran? Was she Lutheran?"

"She doesn't remember."

"Does she remember the name of the minister?"

"Thorpe."

"Thorpe?"

"Yes. Thorpe."

"What was his first name?"

"Thomas Thorpe."

"And when they were married, was that in this town?"

"No."

"What town was it in?"

"A long way away."

"What was the name of the town?"

"Something like Pickwick . . . a funny name like that . . . it's some kind of a province of a place. A Piccadilly — a province in the country, she says."

"And they came right here after that? Or did they go anywhere else to live?"

"Saco. They went into Saco."

"That's the name of a place?"

"Yes."

"How long did they stay there?"

"Six months in Saco."

"And then?"

"Her husband had a commission."

"What kind of commission?"

"On a whaling ship."

"What was the name of the ship?"

"*St. Catherine*. I see *St. Catherine* or *St. Catherines*."

"And then where did they move to?"

"Port Clyde."

". . . And they stayed here for the rest of their lives?"

"Yes, until he went to sea and didn't come back one time."

"His ship didn't come back?"

"No."

"Does she feel better for having told us this?"

"Oh, yes."

"Tell her that she . . ."

"She says it's a long story."

"Tell her that she need not stay where so much unhappiness has transpired in her life. Tell her her husband is over there . . ."

"Yes."

"Does she understand?"

"Yes, she does."

"Does she want to see him again?"

"Yes."

"Then she must call out to him to come to her. Does she understand that?"

"Yes."

"Then tell her to call out to her husband James, right now."

"He'll take her to Surrey or something like that, he says."

"Surrey."

"Surrey. Some funny name."

"Is it a place?"

"Yes, it is."

"Does she see him?"

"Yes."

"Are they going off together?"

"Yes, I see her leaving, slowly, but she's looking back."

"Tell her to go and not to return here. Tell her to go with love and happiness and in peace. Are they gone?"

"They are going. It's a reunion."

"We wish them well and we send them from this house with our blessings, with our love and compassion, and in peace. Go on, go on. What do you see?"

"They are gone."

And with that, we left the house, having done enough for one day. But the real work was yet to come: corroborating the material Ingrid Beckman had come up with.

I turned to Carol for verification, if possible, of some of the names and data Ingrid had come up with. Carol showed us a book containing maps of the area, and we started to check it out.

"Look," Carol said and pointed at the passage in the book, "this strip of land was owned by John Barter and it was right next to Samuel Gardner . . . and it says John Barter died in 1820 . . . the date mentioned by Ingrid! Ah, and there is also mention of the same Margaret Barter, and there is a date on the same page, November 23, 1882 . . . I guess that is when she died."

"Great," I said, pleased to get all this verification

so relatively easily. "What exactly is this book?"

"It's a copy of the early records of the town of St. George."

"Isn't that the town right next door?"

"Yes, it is."

"What about the name Hogden or Hayden or Samuel?"

"Samuel Hatton was a sailor and his wife was named Elmira," Carol said, pointing at the book. Ingrid had joined us now as I saw no further need to keep her in the dark regarding verifications — her part of the work was done.

"We must verify that," I said. "Also, was there ever a ship named *St. Catherine* and was it built on the Kennebec River as Ingrid claimed?"

But who would be able to do that? Happily, fate was kind; there was a great expert who knew both the area and history of the towns better than anyone around, and he agreed to receive us. That turned out to be a colorful ex-sailor by the name of Commander Albert Smalley, who received us in his house in St. George — a house, I might add, which was superbly furnished to suggest the bridge of a ship. After we had stopped admiring his mementos, and made some chitchat to establish the seriousness of our mission, I turned to the commander and put the vital questions to him directly.

"Commander Albert Smalley, you've been a resident in this town for how long?"

"I was born in this town seventy-six years ago."

"I understand you know more about the history of Port Clyde than anybody else."

"Well, that's a moot question, but I will say, possibly, yes."

"Now, to the best of your knowledge, do the names Samuel and Hatton mean anything in connection with this area?"

"Yes, I know Hatton lived at Port Clyde prior to 1850. That I'm sure about."

"What profession did he have?"

"Sailor."

"Was there a ship named the *St. Catherine* in these parts?"

"Yes, there was."

"And would it have been built at the Kennebec River? Or connected with it in some way?"

"Well, as I recall it was, and I believe it was built in the Sewell Yard at the Kennebec River."

"Was there any farming in a small way in the Port Clyde area in the nineteenth century?"

"Oh yes, primarily that's what they came here for. But fishing, of course, was a prime industry."

"Now there's a lighthouse not far from Port Clyde which I believe was built in the early part of the nineteenth century. Could it have been there in the eighteen forties?"

"Yes. It was built in eighteen thirty-three."

"Now if somebody would have been alive in eighteen forty, would they somehow be concerned about this comparatively new lighthouse? Would it have worried them?"

"No, it would not. The residence is comparatively new. The old stone residence was destroyed by lightning. But the tower is the same one."

"Now you know the area of Port Clyde where the Leah Davis house now stands? Prior to this house, were there any houses in the immediate area?"

"I've always been told that there was a house there. The Davis that owned it told me that he built on an old cellar."

"And how far back would that go?"

"That would go back to probably eighteen seventy. The new house was built around eighteen seventy."

"And was there one before that?"

"Yes, there was one before that."

"Could that have been a farmhouse?"

"Yes, it could have been because there is a little farm in back of it. It's small."

"Now you of course have heard all kinds of stories — some of them true, some of them legendary. Have you ever heard any story of a great tragedy concerning the owners of the farmhouse on that point?"

"Whit Thompson used to tell some weird ghost stories. But everyone called him a damned liar. Whether it's true or not, I don't know, but I've heard them."

"About that area?"

"About that area."

"Was there, sir, any story about a female ghost — a woman?"

"I have heard of a female ghost. Yes, Whit used to tell that story."

"What did he tell you?"

"That was a long time ago, and I cannot recall

just what he said about it — he said many things — but she used to appear, especially on foggy nights, and it was hard to distinguish her features — that was one of the things he used to tell about — and there was something about her ringing the bell at the lighthouse, when they used to ring the old fog bell there. I don't recall what it was."

"Now the story we found involved a woman wearing a white gown, looking out to sea from the window as if she were expecting her sailor to return, and she apparently was quite faceless at first."

"I don't think Whitney ever told of her face being seen."

"Do you know of anybody in your recollection who has actually had an unusual experience in that particular area?"

"No, I don't."

"Commander, if you had the choice of spending the night in the house, would it worry you?"

"No, why should it?"

"You are not afraid of ghosts?"

"No. Why should I be?"

"They are people after all."

"Huh?"

"They are just people after all."

"Yes."

"Have you ever seen one?"

"No, I was brought up with mediums and spiritualists and as a kid I was frightened half to death. I didn't dare go out after dark, but I got over that."

"Thank you very much."

"The lighthouse and the gale . . . the ship in a

gale . . . it all seems to fit . . . ," Ingrid mumbled as we got back into our cars and left the commander's house.

And there you have it. A girl from the big city who knows nothing about the case I am investigating, nor where she might be taken, and still comes up with names and data she could not possibly know on her own. Ingrid Beckman was (and is, I suppose) a gifted psychic. Shortly after we finished taping the Port Clyde story, I left for Europe.

While I was away, Ingrid met a former disc jockey then getting interested in the kind of work she and I had been doing so successfully for a while. Somehow he persuaded her to give a newspaper interview about this case — which, of course, upset NBC a lot since this segment would not air for six months, not to mention myself. The newspaper story was rather colorful, making it appear that Ingrid had heard of this ghost and taken care of it . . . but then newspaper stories sometimes distort things, or perhaps the verification and research of a ghost story is less interesting to them than the story itself. But to a professional like myself, the evidence only becomes evidence when it is carefully verified. I haven't worked with Ingrid since.

As for the ghostly lady of Port Clyde, nothing further has been heard about her, either, and since we gently persuaded her not to hang on any longer, chances are indeed that she has long been joined by her man, sailing an ocean where neither gales nor nosy television crews can intrude.

# 11
# The Ghost of Betsy Jumel

One of the most recent hauntings in one of America's most-famous eighteenth-century mansions has fascinated visitors for years — hoping to meet the ghost in person!

It all started with an article in the *New York Journal-American* on January 11, 1964, by Joan Hanauer, in which the ghostly goings-on at Jumel Mansion in New York City were brought to public attention. Youngsters on a field trip from P.S. 164, Edgecombe Avenue and 164th Street, said a tall, gray-haired, elderly woman stepped out onto the balcony and told them to be quiet.

The description fit Madame Jumel.

Could it have happened?

Mrs. Emma Bingay Campbell, curator of the Mansion at 160th Street and Edgecombe, said no.

"I don't believe in ghosts," she said, "but it was very strange. The house was locked and empty. We know that. There could not have been a woman there. But several of the children insist they saw and heard her.

"It was shortly before eleven, opening time for the house, which dates back to 1765.

"When I came over to the children to explain they must wait for John Duffy, the second gardener, to unlock the doors at eleven," Mrs. Campbell said, "one of the girls wanted to know why the tall woman who had come out on the balcony to reprimand them for boisterousness couldn't let them in. There couldn't have been any such woman — or anyone else — in the house.

"The woman the children described resembled Madame Jumel, who some thought murdered her husband in the house in 1832, then married Aaron Burr the following year.

"But the children couldn't know that, or what she looked like.

"They also couldn't know that the balcony on which the apparition appeared separated Madame Jumel's and Burr's bedrooms."

Elizabeth Byrd was then working on a story about Manhattan ghosts for a magazine, so we decided to follow up this case together. First we contacted the public school authorities and obtained permission to talk to the children. The teacher assembled the entire group she had originally taken to the Jumel Mansion, and we questioned them, separately and together. Their story was unchanged. The woman appeared on the balcony, suddenly, and she told them to be quiet.

"How did she disappear?" I wanted to know.

One youngster thought for a moment, then said hesitantly, "She sort of glided back into the house."

"Did you see the balcony doors open?" I asked the girl.

"No, sir," she replied firmly.

"Then did she glide through the door?"

"She did."

The dress they described the ghost as wearing does exist — but it is put away carefully upstairs in the mansion and was not on display, nor is this common knowledge, especially among eleven-year-old schoolgirls.

There was a cooking class in progress when we arrived, and the girls cheerfully offered us samples of their art. We declined for the moment and went on to see the curator of the mansion, Mrs. Campbell. This energetic lady takes care of the mansion for the Daughters of the American Revolution in whose charge the City of New York had placed the museum.

"Is this the first report of a haunting here?" I wanted to know.

Mrs. Campbell shook her head. "Here," she said, and took down from one of the shelves in her office a heavy book. "William Henry Shelton's work, *The Jumel Mansion*, pages two hundred seven and two hundred eight report earlier ghosts observed here."

"Have you ever seen or heard anything?"

"No, not yet, but others have. There was that German nurse who lived here in eighteen sixty-five — she heard strange noises even then. Footsteps have been heard by many visitors here when there was no one about. The ghost of Madame Jumel appeared to a retired guard at the door of this room."

"How would you like me to investigate the matter?" I offered. A date was set immediately.

First, I thought it wise to familiarize myself with the physical layout of the historic house. I was immediately struck by its imposing appearance. Historian John Kent Tilton wrote:

> Located on the highest elevation of Manhattan is one of the most famous old historic houses in the nation, the Morris-Jumel Mansion. The locality was originally called Haarlem Heights by the Dutch in the days of New Amsterdam and was then changed to Mount Morris during the English ownership, before receiving the present name of Washington Heights.
>
> The plot of land upon which the old mansion is situated was originally deeded in 1700 to a Dutch farmer named Jan Kiersen, from part of the "half morgen of land of the common woods" of New Haarlem.
>
> Lieutenant Colonel Roger Morris purchased the estate in 1765. The new owner was born in England in 1728 and came to America at the age of eighteen with a commission of captaincy in the British army.
>
> It was here that the Morris family, with their four children, spent their summers, living the domestic life typical of a British squire

and family until the outbreak of the Revolution.

Colonel Morris fled to England at the beginning of hostilities, where he remained for two and one-half years.

As early in the war as August 1776, Mount Morris was taken over by the American troops, and General Heath and staff were quartered there. After the disastrous Battle of Long Island, General Washington retreated to Haarlem Heights and made the place his headquarters. After Washington decided to abandon this location, the British moved in and the Morris Mansion housed General Sir Henry Clinton and his officers and, at intervals, the Hessians, during the seven years the British occupied New York.

During the following quarter of a century it was sold and resold several times and witnessed many changes in its varied career. Renamed Calumet Hall, it served for a time as a tavern and was a stopping place for the stage coaches en route to Albany. It was the home of an unknown farmer when President Washington paid a visit to his old headquarters and entertained at dinner, among others, his cabinet members, John Adams, Alexander Hamilton, Henry Knox, and their wives.

The locality was one that Stephen Jumel with his sprightly and ambitious wife delighted driving out to on a summer's day from their home on Whitehall Street. Mme. Jumel became entranced with the nearby old Morris Mansion and persuaded her husband to purchase it for their home in 1810, for the sum of $10,000 which included 35 acres of land still remaining of the original tract.

The old house was fast falling into decay when Mme. Jumel energetically went about renovating and refurnishing it, and when completed, it was one of the most beautiful homes in the country. The Jumels restored the mansion in the style of the early nineteenth century, when the Federal influence was in fashion.

Mme. Jumel first married, some say by trickery, the rich Frenchman, Stephen Jumel. He had at one time owned a large plantation in Santo Domingo from whence he was obliged to flee at the time of the insurrection. Arriving in the United States, a comparatively poor man, he soon amassed a new fortune as a wine merchant, and at his death in 1832, his wife became one of the richest women in America. A year later she married Aaron Burr, former vice president of the United States. This second marriage, however, was of short duration and ended in divorce. Mme. Jumel died at the age of 93 in 1865.

The Morris-Jumel mansion is of the mid-Georgian period of architecture. The front facade has four columns, two stories in height, with a pediment at the top.

The exterior is painted white. One of the post-Colonial features added by the Jumels is the imposing front entrance doorway, with flanking sidelights and elliptical fanlight.

In the interior, the wide central hall with arches is furnished with late-eighteenth- and early-nineteenth-century pieces. At the left of the entrance is the small parlor or tearoom where the marriage ceremony of the Widow Jumel and Aaron Burr was performed in 1833 when the bride was fifty-eight and the groom twenty years her senior.

Across the hall is the stately Georgian dining room where many persons of fame assembled for elaborate dinner parties.

At the rear of the hall is the large octagonal drawing room.

The broad stairway leads to the spacious hall on the upper floor, which is furnished with personal belongings of the Jumels. There is a group portrait of Madame Jumel and the young son and daughter of her adopted daughter, Mary Eliza, who married Nelson Chase.

The northwest bedroom contains furniture owned by the Jumels, including a carved four-poster bed.

In the old days the rooms on the third floor were probably used as extra guest chambers since the servants' quarters were then located in the basement with the kitchen.

On January 19, 1964, a small group of people assembled in Betsy Jumel's old sitting room upstairs. Present were a few members of the New York Historical Society and the Daughters of the American Revolution, *Journal-American* writer Nat Adams, and late-comer Harry Altschuler of the *World-Telegram*. I was accompanied by Ethel Meyers, who had not been told where we were going that winter afternoon, and Jessyca Russell Gaver, who was serving as my secretary and doing a magazine article on our work at the same time.

We had barely arrived when Ethel went in and out of the Jumel bedroom as if someone were forcing her to do so. As she approached the room across the hall, her shoulder sagged and one arm hung loose as if her side had been injured!

"I feel funny on my left side," Ethel finally said, and her voice had already taken on some of the coloring of someone else's.

We went back to the bedroom, which is normally closed to the public. One side is occupied by a huge carved four-poster, once the property of Napoleon I, and there are small chairs of the period in various spots throughout the room. In one corner, there is a large mirror.

"The issue is confused," Ethel said, and sounded confused herself. "There is more than one disturbed person here. I almost feel as though three people were involved. There has been sickness and a change of heart. Someone got a raw deal."

Suddenly, Ethel turned to one of the men who had sat down on Napoleon's bed. "Someone wants you to get up from that bed," she said, and evinced difficulty in speaking. As if bitten by a tarantula, the young man shot up from the bed.

Ethel again struggled to her feet, despite my restraining touch on her arm. "I've got to go back to that other room again," she mumbled, and off she went, with me trailing after her. She walked almost as if she were being taken over by an outside force. In front of the picture of Madame Jumel, she suddenly fell to her knees.

"I never can go forward here. . . . I fall whenever I'm near there." She pointed at the large picture above her, and almost shouted, "My name isn't on that picture. I want my name there!"

Mrs. Campbell, the curator, took me aside in agitation. "That's very strange she should say that," she remarked. "You see, her name really used to be on that picture a long time ago. But that picture wasn't in this spot when Betsy Jumel was alive."

I thanked her and led Ethel Meyers back to her chair in the other room.

"Henry . . . and a Johann . . . around her . . . ," she mumbled as she started to go into a deep trance. Hoarse sounds emanated from her lips. At first they were unintelligible. Gradually I was able to make them out. Halfway into a trance, she moved over to the bed and lay down on it. I placed my chair next to her head. The others strained to hear. There was an eerie silence about the room, interrupted only by the soft words of the entranced medium.

"You think me dead . . ." a harsh, male voice now said.

"No, I've come to talk to you, to help you," I replied.

"Go away," the ghostly voice said. "Go away!"

"Are you a man or a woman?" I asked.

A bitter laugh was the reply.

"Man . . . ha!" the voice finally said.

"What is your name?"

"Everybody knows who I am."

"I don't. What is your name?" I repeated.

"Let me sleep."

"Is anything troubling you?"

There was a moment of silence, then the voice was a bit softer. "Who are *you?*"

"I'm a friend come to help you."

"Nobody talks to me. They think I'm dead."

"What exactly happened to you?"

"They took me away," the voice said in plaintive tones. "I am not dead yet. Why did they take me away?"

Now the body of the medium shook as if in great agitation, while I spoke soothing words to calm the atmosphere. Suddenly, the ghost speaking through the medium was gone, and in his place was the crisp, matter-of-fact voice of Albert, Ethel's control. I asked Albert to tell us through the entranced medium who the ghost was.

"I don't hear a name, but I see a sturdy body and round face. He complains he was pronounced dead when he in fact wasn't. I believe he is the owner of the house and it bears his name. There are many jealousies in this house. There is an artist who is also under suspicion."

"Is there a woman here?"

"One thwarted of what she desired and who

wants to throw herself out the window."

"Why?" I asked.

"Thwarted in love and under suspicion."

Later, I asked Mrs. Campbell about this. She thought for a moment, then confirmed the following facts: A young servant girl involved with one of the family tried to commit suicide by jumping out the window.

I questioned Albert further. "Is there a restless woman in this house?"

"That is right. The one in the picture. Her conscience disturbs her."

"About what?"

The medium now grabbed her side, as if in pain. "I am being threatened," Albert said now. "I feel the revelation would disturb."

"But how can I release her unless I know what is holding her here?"

"It has to do with the death of her husband. That he was strangled in his coffin."

I tried to question him further, but he cut us short. The medium had to be released now.

Soon, Ethel Meyers was back to her own self. She remembered very little of the trance, but her impressions of a clairvoyant nature continued for a while. I queried her about the person on the bed.

"I get the initial J," she replied and rubbed her side.

I turned to Mrs. Campbell. "What about the story of Madame Jumel's guilty conscience?"

"Well," the curator replied, "after her husband's death, she refused to live in this house for some time. She always felt guilty about it."

We were standing in a corner where the medium could not hear us. "Stephen Jumel bled to death from a wound he had gotten in a carriage accident. Madame Jumel allegedly tore off his bandage and let him die. That much we know."

Mrs. Campbell naturally is a specialist on Betsy Jumel and her life, and she knows many intimate details unknown to the general public or even to researchers.

It was five-thirty in the afternoon when we left the house, which must be closed for the night after that hour.

The next morning two newspaper accounts appeared: One, fairly accurate, in the *Journal*, and a silly one in the *Telegram*, by a man who stood outside the room of the investigation and heard very little, if anything.

Several weeks went by and my ghost-hunting activities took me all over the country. Then I received a telephone call from Mrs. Campbell.

"Did you know that May twenty-second is the anniversary of Stephen Jumel's death?" I didn't and I wagered her nobody else did, except herself and the late Mr. Jumel. She allowed as to that and suggested we have another go at the case on that date. I have always felt that anniversaries are good times to solve murder cases so I readily agreed.

This time, the *Journal* and *Telegram* reporters weren't invited, but *The New York Times*, in the person of reporter Grace Glueck, was, and I am indebted to her for the notes she took of the proceedings that warm May afternoon.

Present also were the general manager of King Features, Frank McLearn; Clark Kinnaird, literary critic of the *Journal*; John Allen and Bob O'Brien of *Reader's Digest*; Emeline Paige, the editor of *The Villager*; writers Elizabeth Byrd and Beverly Balin; Ed Joyce of CBS; and several members of the New York Historical Society, presumably there as observers ready to rewrite history as needed since the famous Aaron Burr might be involved.

Ethel Meyers was told nothing about the significance of the date, nor had I discussed with her the results of the first séance.

Again we assembled in the upstairs bedroom and Ed Joyce set up his tape recorder in front of Napoleon's bed, while Ethel sat on the bed itself and I next to her on a chair. To my left, the young lady from the *Times* took her seat. All in all there must have been twenty-five anxious people in the room, straining to hear all that was said and keeping a respectful silence when asked to. Within a few minutes, Ethel was in a deep trance, and a male voice spoke through her vocal cords.

"Who are you?" I asked as I usually do when an unknown person comes through a medium.

"*Je suis Stephen*," the voice said.

"Do you speak English?"

In answer, the medium clutched at her body and groaned. "Doctor! Doctor! Where is the doctor?"

"What is hurting you?" I asked.

The voice was firm and defiant now. "I'm alive, I'm alive . . . don't take me away."

"Did you have an accident? What happened to you?"

"She tricked me."

"Who tricked you?"

"I can't breathe . . . where is she? She tricked me. Look at her!"

"Don't worry about her," I said. "She's dead."

"But I'm alive!" the entranced voice continued.

"In a sense, you are. But you have also passed over."

"No — they put me in the grave when I was not yet dead."

"How did you get hurt?" I wanted to know.

The ghost gave a bitter snort. "What matter — I'm dead. You said so."

"I didn't say you were dead," I replied.

The voice became furious again. "She took it, she took it — that woman. She took my life. Go away."

"I'm your friend."

"I haven't any friends . . . that Aaron . . ."

"Aaron? Was he involved in your death?"

"That strumper . . . hold him! They buried me alive, I tell you."

"When did this happen?"

"It was cold. She made me a fool, a fool!"

"How did she do that?"

"All the time I loved her, she tricked me."

"I want to help you."

"I'm bleeding."

"How did this happen?"

"Pitchfork . . . wagon . . . hay . . ."

"Was it an accident, yes or no?"

"I fell on it."

"You fell on the pitchfork?"

"Look at the blood bath . . . on Napoleon's bed."

"What about that pitchfork?" I insisted.

"There was a boy in the hay, and he pushed me off."

"Did you know this boy?"

"Yes . . . give me *her*. She wanted to be a lady. I saw it. I wasn't so foolish I didn't see it."

"What happened when you got home?"

"She told me I was going to die."

"Did you have a doctor?"

"Yes."

"Wasn't the wound bandaged?"

"They took me out alive. I was a live man he put in the grave. I want to be free from that grave!"

"Do you want me to set you free?"

"God bless you!"

"It is your hatred that keeps you here. You must forgive."

"She did it to me."

I then pleaded with the ghost to join his own family and let go of his memories. "Do you realize how much time has gone on since? A hundred years!"

"Hundred years!"

The medium, still entranced, buried her head in her hands: "I'm mad!"

"Go from this house and don't return."

"Mary, Mary!"

Mary was the name of Jumel's daugher, a fact not known to the medium at the time.

"Go and join Mary!" I commanded, and asked that Albert, the control, help the unhappy one find the way.

Just as soon as Jumel's ghost had left us, someone else slipped into the medium's body, or so it seemed, for she sat up and peered at us with a suspicious expression. "Who are you?"

"I'm a friend, come to help," I replied.

"I didn't ask for you."

"My name is Holzer, and I have come to seek you out. If you have a name worth mentioning, please tell us!"

"Get out or I'll call the police! This is my house."

"There was real anger now on the medium's entranced face.

I kept asking for identification. Finally, the disdainful lips opened and in cold tones, the voice said, "I am the wife of the vice president of the United States! Leave my house!"

I checked with Mrs. Campbell and found that Betsy Jumel did so identify herself frequently. On one occasion, driving through crowded New York streets long after her divorce from Aaron Burr, she shouted, "Make way for the wife of the vice president of the United States!"

"Didn't you marry someone else before that?" I asked. "How did your husband die?"

"You are made like the billow in the captain's

cabin," she replied, somewhat cryptically. Later I checked this out. A sea captain was one of her favorite lovers while married to Jumel.

"Did you murder your husband?" I inquired and drew back a little just in case.

"You belong in the scullery with my maids," she replied disdainfully.

I repeated the accusation, adding that her husband had claimed she had killed him.

"I will call for help," she countered.

"There is no help. The police are on your trail!" I suggested.

"I am the wife of the vice president of the United States!"

"I will help you if you tell me what you did. Did you cause his death?"

"The rats that crawl . . . they bit me. Where am I?"

"You're between two worlds. Do you wish to be helped?"

"Where is Joseph?"

"You must leave this house. Your husband has forgiven you."

"I adored him!"

"Go away, and you will see Stephen Jumel again."

"Only the crest on the carriage! That's all I did. He was a great man."

I had the feeling she wasn't at all keen on Monsieur Jumel. But that happens, even to ghosts.

I finally gave up trying to get her to go and join Jumel and tried another way.

"Go and join the vice president of the United States. He awaits you." To my surprise, this didn't work either.

"He is evil, evil," she said.

Perplexed, I asked, "Whom do you wish to join?"

"Mary."

"Then call out her name, and she'll join you and take you with her."

"No crime, no crime."

"You've been forgiven. Mary will take you away from here."

I asked Albert, the control, to come and help us get things moving, but evidently Madame had a change of heart: "This is my house. I'll stay here."

"This is no longer your house. You must go!"

The struggle continued. She called for Christopher, but wouldn't tell me who Christopher was.

"He's the only one I ever trusted," she volunteered, finally.

"It's not too late," I repeated. "You can join your loved ones."

"Good-bye."

I called for Albert, who quickly took control. "She's no longer in the right mind," he said, as soon as he had firm control of the medium's vocal cords. "You may have to talk with her again."

"Is she guilty of Jumel's death?"

"Yes. It was arranged."

"Who was the boy who pushed him?"

"A trusty in the house. She told him to."

"What about Stephen Jumel?"

"He is in a better frame of mind."

"Is there anything else we did not bring out? Who is this Christopher she mentioned?"

"A sea captain. She buried him in Providence."

Mrs. Campbell later confirmed the important role the sea captain played in Betsy's life. There was also another man named Brown.

"Did Aaron Burr help bury Jumel?"

"That is true. Burr believed Madame Jumel had more finances than she actually had."

"What about the doctor who buried him alive? Is his name known?"

"Couldn't stop the bleeding."

"Was Aaron Burr in on the crime?"

"He is very much aware that he is guilty. He still possesses his full mental faculties."

I then asked the control to help keep the peace in the house and to bring the medium back to her own body.

A few minutes later, Ethel Meyers was herself again, remembering nothing of the ordeal she had gone through the past hour, and none the worse for it.

Jumel died in 1832 and, as far as I could find, the first ghostly reports date back to 1865. The question was: Could his remains disclose any clues as to the manner in which he died? If he suffocated in his coffin, would not the position of his bones so indicate?

I queried two physicians who disagreed in the matter. One thought that nothing would be left by now; the other thought it was worth looking into.

I thought so, too. However, my application to

reopen the grave of Stephen Jumel, down in the old Catholic cemetery on Mott Street, got the official run-around. The district attorney's office sent me to Dr. Halpern, the chief medical examiner, who told me it would be of no use to check. When I insisted, I was referred to the church offices of old St. Patrick's, which has nominal jurisdiction over the plot.

Have you ever tried to reopen a grave in the City of New York? It's easier to dig a new one, believe me!

As the years passed, I often returned to the mansion. I made several television documentaries there with the helpful support of the curator, who now is the affable and knowledgeable Patrick Broom. The famous blue gown is no longer on display, alas, having disintegrated shortly after I first published the story. But the legend persists, and the footfalls are still heard on lonely nights when the security guard locks up.

# 12
# The Haunted Stagecoach Inn

I owe this lead to Mrs. Gwen Hinzie, a devoted fan of mine.

Mrs. Gwen Hinzie, my San Francisco "ghost scout," and psychic herself, this time had really done some useful spadework.

In an area like California, where so much violence has taken place not only during the nineteenth-century pioneer days but in comparatively recent times, psychic occurrences are not at all unlikely, and I only asked that there be some specific "complaint." There was.

We then drove to the Stagecoach Inn, a handsome mid-nineteenth-century building originally erected as a way station when this spot was a major factor in the stagecoach route to and from California. Later, it had deteriorated into an inn, the kind that takes on all comers and does not ask too many questions just so long as they can pay their bills.

According to Guy Runnion, editor of the *Conejo*

*News* and the unofficial historian of this landmark, there had been killings here, and as far back as the 1930s, reports of hauntings at the inn were prevalent.

A Mr. Dyke of nearby Thousand Oaks confirmed that his own father, a well-driller during those years, had spoken to him of such goings-on.

At present, the inn is a museum, and it has just been moved on its foundations to a new location a few yards farther back from the original site to allow the freeway to pass. Whether the alleged ghost or ghosts would resent the move, or move out themselves, was a moot point — for me to find out.

The historical society in the person of Dr. Cyril Anderson has charge of the buildings now.

From 1952 to 1965, however, it had been used as a giftshop by a couple named McIntyre who spoke of a female ghost there; however, when questioned, Mrs. Kenneth McIntyre passed the matter off as "just a story" without substance.

When Gwen Hinzie was doing newspaper work in the area in 1962, she had occasion to visit the inn frequently since it is only a few blocks away from the Hinzie house. The land, in fact, is really one and the same parcel, connected with both the hill on which the Hinzie house now stands and the entire Hays family holdings around it. That this was of some significance we were to learn a little later.

But when Mrs. Hinzie first entered the 19-room mansion, Mrs. McIntyre remarked how odd it was that Mrs. Hinzie's hair should suddenly stand on end. Evidently hair raising is to Mrs. Hinzie what goose pimples are to Sybil Leek: an indicator of psychic energies in the area.

At this moment, Mrs. Hinzie heard a crash upstairs, but she was assured by the proprietor of the giftshop that there was nobody there. But her curiosity was aroused and she next talked to Donna Fargo, of the famous Wells-Fargo family, regarding the Inn. Bandits, it seems, were roving in this area during stagecoach days, and only twenty miles away at Colahasas, things were truly "wild west."

The inn had been built in the expectancy of a great deal of business because of the Butterfield mail route which was supposed to have gone through the Conejo Valley on the way to St. Louis; and there was already a post office at Newbury Park in 1875. But the Civil War interfered and the Butterfield line declined in importance, as the main route went through the Santa Clara Valley instead.

We arrived at the house while the sun was blazing, and the coolness of the inside was a welcome relief from its unremitting rays. The work of restoration was in full progress, but one could see that the house had had some stature at one time; it reminded one of the typical Western gambling inn movie set, complete with stairway leading to the rooms upstairs.

Sybil had started to "putter around," and I took great care to point out the various pitfalls where she might have landed in the basement without benefit of stairs. But Sybil is agile, and her five senses, not to mention her sixth, kept her out of trouble.

I found her in a room to the left of the stairs, a

room that undoubtedly was once a guest room when the inn was a hotel.

"This room interests me," Sybil explained, "more than the rest of the house. Before we arrived I had a feeling of something very unstable. Well, it is. The foundations are not ready. The house has been moved. Also, I feel a connection with the other place as if this were in line with it."

I realized that the land was of one piece. Was Sybil picking up the Indian trail again?

"What sort of place do you feel this is?" As always, I had not told Sybil anything about the place we were in at the moment. It could be a private house, a manor, anything; there was nothing to indicate that it was an inn, especially a stagecoach inn. And yet Sybil got the scent.

"A meeting place . . . not just a residence. Too many people come and go and leave disturbances . . . food and drink place. . . ."

Meanwhile, Leighton Field, a photographer with the Historical Society, and Kathy Berg, a young lady reporter from the *News-Chronicle*, had arrived and followed us around in the hope of catching, if not a ghost, at least some interesting conversation.

"I'm very depressed," Sybil now said, "especially in this room . . . tragedy . . . perhaps the room above also. . . ."

We entered the upstairs room and Sybil picked up something stronger now.

"Think of the name Pierre Devon," Sybil suggested, "that is the name that is there . . . 1882 to 1889 . . . violent headache . . . right hand side of head . . . died here . . . still present in this part of the house . . . short, dirty, not a farmer, mountains . . . passing through . . . passing through before Los Angeles . . . *hidalgo*. . . . What does it mean?"

"That means *gentleman*," said the curator, who had come up to us. "The house was built in 1876, so it was here in 1882."

But despite a careful search of the fragmentary records still extant about the period in question, no Pierre Devon could be pinned down. If this man was merely a transient passenger, spending a night here en route to Los Angeles, there hardly would be any. And if some local murderers had relieved him of his gold, there would be even less reason to let the world know.

Thus it appears that Pierre Devon, whoever he was, has taken the secret of his demise with him. I only hope that seeing Sybil, and being briefly aware of the outside world through her, will have sufficiently shaken him to allow him to leave the place of his death. Now that the inn has been moved back from the original site, he really has no reason to stay on. Who ever heard of a ghost sitting on the freeway? He'd get himself killed all over again!

# 13
# The Ghost of "Ocean-Born" Mary

In one of the most beautiful parts of New Hampshire, there is a truly impressive New England mansion known nowadays as the Ocean-Born Mary House, a name which has stuck to it ever since it was built by a certain Mary Wallace who was born aboard ship while crossing over to the New World. I have been to the Ocean-Born Mary House several times and conducted three separate investigations there with two different mediums, and the material was truly astounding. So were the eyewitness accounts of those who have seen a ghost in the house or at the window. Nevertheless, because neighborhood youths kept making the house a target for their Halloween pranks, the owners began to shy away from the true story and eventually told eager tourists that there was nothing to the ghosts after all and to please not bother them. Thus if you intend visiting the Ocean-Born Mary House in Henniker, New Hampshire, about an hour's ride out of Boston, do so because you want to visit an historical mansion and do not bring up the matter of ghosts with the present owners for they may not wish to admit you.

Mary was befriended by a pirate, Don Pedro. Later in life he helped her build this house, and in turn she permitted him to spend his old age there. Unfortunately for Don Pedro, so the story goes, one of his men who had been angry with him caught up with him, and in the ensuing fight Don Pedro was killed. Allegedly his body lies underneath the fireplace, but there is no proof since the fireplace has never been dug up.

The place came to my attention when a local amateur medium, Mrs. A., asked my assistance in dealing with the phenomena she had encountered at the house. During a routine visit as a tourist, she had found herself practically taken over by the spirit of Mary Wallace who demanded to be heard through her. Frightened, she fled home to a Boston suburb. That night she awoke and, without being able to resist, drove her car all the way back up to New Hampshire, still in her nightclothes.

I brought Mrs. A. back to Ocean-Born Mary's with me, in the daytime and wearing street clothes, and, in trance, Mary Wallace manifested. The gist of her communication through the medium was a concern for the proper maintenance of the old house and an almost playful desire to be acknowledged and recognized.

Subsequent to this visit I also drove up with Sybil Leek and attempted another trance session. Sybil managed to bring through a servant girl who had apparently met with foul play or was involved in it. At any rate, she must be the third resident ghost, in addition to Mary Wallace and her pirate friend.

There was also talk of a buried treasure somewhere on the grounds. The directions were quite explicit and, after Sybil came out of trance, we all went out and looked for the treasure underneath the stones behind the house. We did not dig, of course, and treasures have a way of staying underground, especially after two hundred fifty years.

While there may be some speculation about the reality of the hidden treasure and possibly of the continued residence "in spirit" of the pirate, there is substantial evidence that the house is haunted by a woman greatly resembling the original owner.

A number of people have seen the tall, stately figure of Mary Wallace peering out of an upstairs window of the two-story structure. It was her favorite place, and from the description given there is no doubt that those who saw the figure were indeed seeing the ghost of Mary Wallace.

On one occasion, her intervention saved the house from burning to the ground. A heater had caught fire, but was smothered by unseen hands. The ghost has been described by one who saw her as "a lovely lady in her thirties with auburn-colored hair, smiling rather intensely and thoughtfully."

On another occasion, two state troopers saw her walking down the road leading up to the house, wearing a Colonial-type costume, and a casual visitor to the house was shown around by a tall lady at a time when the owners were away. Only later did this visitor realize that it had been Mary Wallace who had been so hospitable.

The house can be reached by car from Boston. It is worth a visit. If you are wondering about the reality of pirates in the late-eighteenth century in this area, be assured that it was not uncommon for such men of the sea to retire to their beloved New England, to settle down at a safe distance from the sea. There are other mansions and manor houses in the area which owe their existence to the wealth accumulated by sea captains, some of them of doubtful honesty, but nevertheless, if it weren't for them, these houses would have never been built. Thus we do owe Don Pedro a debt of gratitude for having caused Mary Wallace to erect this beautiful New England mansion.

# 14
# The Ghost in the Closet

Nowadays lots of things come out of the closet other than clothes — secrets, hidden stories, long-lost papers — but this is about a ghost who liked the closet he was in so much he did not want to come out of it at all.

It all started when I was lecturing for the American Society for Psychic Research in Los Angeles, and a good many people came forward to tell of their own psychic experiences, especially those involving ghosts and apparitions. In fact, so many people attended this lecture, and so many more got in touch with me afterwards about their own experiences, that the Society got worried about it, and I haven't spoken for them since. Small wonder, for I never mince words and I don't send my audience home wondering if the speaker really believes what he is telling his public. My cases are well-documented.

One of the people who could not get to hear me speak was a lady named Verna Kunze. She had seen a ghost, and I asked her to make a written statement about her experience. A practical and factual woman, Mrs. Kunze did not hesitate to do so.

"I had purchased an apartment building in San Bernardino, California, on G Street, which had formerly been a nun's home on E Street closer in town. Undoubtedly it had been a single dwelling mansion at one time.

"The upper-right-hand apartment was more suited to my needs and the one I was occupying during the time — September 1957 to October 1960.

"After I had lived there for some months I came in from a shopping trip and, going to the closet in the front bedroom, opened the door to hang up my coat. There I saw very clearly, standing inside the closet behind the door, a man of medium height (about 5′ 8″), round face, fair complexion, dressed in clothing about the style of the early 1900s, pink-and-white-striped shirt, no coat, high stiff turned-over collar, sailor straw hat on his head, nondescript tan trousers and button shoes — I think they were brown with white trim. Garters to hold up his sleeves were on his arms.

"At first I was so startled (not scared) that I couldn't say anything, but while I was staring at him the picture faded from sight.

"I saw him again in the same position, same clothing, in exactly the same manner on three other occasions.

"Being rather psychic but not a medium, I asked

the Supreme Deity for protection and thought nothing of it. After about the third appearance, I asked that he depart, asked God's blessing on him and saw him no more. However, on the last impression, it seemed to me that he might have been murdered and stood in the closet to be hidden — or had committed a murder and was hiding in the closet. He was as clear in picture as though he were real. I told a medium friend about it who visited me a short time later, but no one else.

"Later I sold the apartment and returned to Santa Ana. I do not know who owns the apartment building now as it has changed hands since."

I travel a great deal and it was not until the fall of 1966 that I finally got around to the ghost in San Bernardino. I got in touch with Mrs. Kunze to see if anything had happened, or at any rate if she could arrange for us to visit her old apartment.

Mrs. Kunze went to see the current owners of the house and found them somewhat hesitant about the whole business. They had not received any complaints from anyone about ghosts and would just as well let sleeping ghosts lie. But Mrs. Kunze is a persuasive person, having spent many years working for the immigration service. She promised not to divulge the exact address of the house or the name of the current owners, and finally an appointment was made for us to have a look at the house in October 1966. Fortunately, the tenant of the corner apartment we were interested in had just vacated and the new owner had not yet moved in —

so we would find an empty apartment.

In return for so much spade work, I promised Mrs. Kunze to address the Psynetics Foundation in nearby Santa Ana, a group in which she was active. The visit to their headquarters was a most pleasurable experience.

After we arrived in Los Angeles, I phoned Mrs. Kunze again to make sure we had access to the apartment. All was in readiness, and we arrived at the house on schedule, at four in the afternoon on a hot October day.

The house sat back from the street, a modest yellow stucco building of two stories which belied its age, which was, I later discovered, considerable for this part of the world.

A dark-haired lady received me at the door, while Catherine and Sybil Leek remained in the car, out of earshot. Mrs. Kunze also came out to greet me. I then fetched the others, and without saying anything pertaining to the house, we left the dark-haired lady, who was the landlady, downstairs and walked up to the second floor where we followed Sybil into the "right" apartment. She knew just where to go.

Mrs. Kunze sat down in one of the chairs, Sybil stretched out on the bed and we waited for what might happen now. We did not have to wait long, for Sybil instantly got the scent of things.

"Death and destruction," she said, "comparatively recent. This is an absolutely horrible place."

She shivered, though the temperature outside was above 90 degrees. I, too, felt a chill, and it wasn't the power of suggestion, either.

"I think death has hung over this place for some time," Sybil elaborated now. "If there was anyone in it I would warn them not to be here."

"Is any entity present?" I asked casually, for I already knew the place was haunted. What I did not know of course was the story behind the haunting or anything more than what Mrs. Kunze had originally written me. And Sybil had no knowledge even of that.

"I seem to be attracted to the bathroom and that little door there," Sybil commented. "The bathroom has some significance in this. Stomach feels irritated."

"What about any structural changes?" I interjected.

"I haven't paid attention to that, for the overwhelming influence is of terribly brooding, resentful . . . death. Like having my head in a piece of *black velvet*. Something hanging right over me."

"Does it involve violent death?"

"Yes. Suffocation. But then again, I have this sickness of the stomach, but that may be associated with someone here. . . ."

"Is it murder, suicide, or accidental death?"

"*Two people* are involved. A murder, because of the resentfulness. Connection with the door. Not clear yet. An usurper, a person who should not be here."

"How far back do we go here?"

"It could be now . . . it seems very close. Recent."

"Describe the person you feel present here."

"A slightly round-faced lady . . . funny, I keep getting another house!"

Sybil interrupted herself. She knew nothing of the fact that this house had been moved to its present site from another place.

"Where is the other house?" I asked.

"The person who is here was involved with *another* house. Tall, thin trees nearby. Two houses . . . the other is a pleasant house . . . light-colored car. . . ."

I asked Sybil to look at the woman again, if she could.

"Hair short in neck. . . ." Sybil said, gradually becoming more and more in trance. "I can't find the body, though . . . one part of her is here and one part of her is there . . ."

"Is she present now?"

"I follow her. . . ."

"Is she in this room?"

"Yes . . . and then she goes . . . D . . . Don . . ."

"What is her occupation?"

"The voice . . . voice . . . she runs away . . . somebody mustn't know, she says . . . she is very vain . . ."

"How is she dressed?"

"Black head," Sybil said. It struck me suddenly that Sybil might be describing a nun's habit.

"Why is the black head here?" Sybil now demanded to know.

But Sybil was speaking of a black *face*.

"Light car, black face," she mumbled.

"Why is she here?" I wanted to know.

"Waiting for . . . this isn't her home. Waiting for relief. Somebody came to take her away from here. A woman. Because she did not live here."

"How did she get here then?"

"She needed to stay here to wait for things . . . to come to her."

"Whose place is this?"

"Don't know . . . knew someone here. The little car, light car. D-o-n."

"What happened to her here?"

"She — was — suffocating — sick to stomach — head and neck —— "

"Did she commit suicide?"

"No."

"Was she murdered?"

"Don't say that!"

"Was she killed?"

"Yes . . ."

"By whom?"

"D-o-n."

"Why did he kill her?"

"From the house . . . somebody made her come here . . ."

I explained, via Sybil, that she must not stay on here. But it did not go down well with the elusive ghost.

"Wants to be alone here," Sybil reported.

"What is troubling her?"

"Mistaken identity. She was . . . misjudged . . . the *other house* . . ."

Had someone accused this woman of something she did not do? Was she a nun?

"Verraco," Sybil said, clearly. It did not ring a bell with Mrs. Kunze, who was observing the proceedings closely. Nor, of course, with me.

"I don't know what it means . . . Verraco," Sybil said.

"Does she realize she is dead?"

"No, she thinks she is sick."

"Can she hear you?"

"She understands, but then she goes away again. I have to go after her."

I asked Sybil to instruct the ghost about her true status.

"Man . . . doesn't trust him," Sybil reported. Had the ghost woman been hurt by a man and did she therefore not trust any other man?

Sybil nodded, that was it. But it was of no avail.

"Go away, she says," Sybil continued, "people upset her, nobody understands what she feels like. Very unhappy woman."

There was a moment of interruption, when I changed tapes. Meanwhile, Sybil startled us with an expression that did not seem to fit in.

"Sing to me," she said, in a drowsy tone, "she was singing . . . she likes music . . . she was misjudged . . . two people, two lives . . . *she was two people . . .*"

I kept coaxing her to confess.

"Suppose he comes back again. . . ." There was terror in Sybil's voice now.

I promised to protect her. She remained doubtful. How did I know?

"I have the power to send him away," I assured her.

"What is the truth about her?"

"The truth is that she did nothing to hurt the woman; that was a misunderstanding."

"Who is the other woman?"

"E.K."

"Where does she live?"

"Verracho." It had been "Verraco" before.

"And Don?"

"Man with light car and dark face."

"Does he know the woman, E.K.?"

"Yes."

"Did she send him here?"

"She knew."

"Was she behind it?"

"She organized it . . . to destroy."

"What is her name . . . the one who is here?"

With ghosts, if you don't succeed at first, try again.

"A.D.," Sybil said softly.

"What year are we in?" I asked.

"Today . . . September . . . 16 . . . '53 . . . lot of people round the house, strange people . . . just looking around . . . she is here watching . . . body in the bathroom. . . ."

Was the ghost re-living the discovery of her body?

"Tell her the world knows that she is innocent," I intoned.

Sybil, still under the spell of the entity, reacted almost violently.

"She *is* innocent!"

I kept reassuring her. Finally, Sybil said: "She will sing . . . A.D. . . . Must not return here ever . . . She is gone now. . . ."

Deeply breathing now, Sybil was completely "out" for a few moments, prior to taking over her own body once again.

I then brought Sybil quickly to herself, but for some time after, she kept feeling quite uncomfortable and sighed with relief when we left the place.

Mrs. Kunze, who had witnessed all this, had nodded several times during the hour. I now wanted to find out if there was anything she could add to the brief testimony she had given me originally.

"Did this apparition you told me about ever look at you?" I inquired. The man with "the German face" in the straw hat must have been quite a sight greeting her from the open closet door — very dead.

"No, he did not," Mrs. Kunze replied. "I immediately got the impression that he was dead. His eyes did not move. A minute later he was gone and I hung up my coat."

A month later, when he reappeared to her, he did not stay as long, she explained, but the view was the same.

The third time she started to pray for him, and instead of fading away as on the previous occasions, he disappeared like a flash.

"Weren't you curious about the apartment? I

mean, didn't you make some inquiries about its previous occupants?"

"I did not. I knew when I bought the place that it had been the home of nuns, and moved here after some years from another location — where the Junior High School now stands. The building is at least sixty years old. There may have been two or three other owners before I purchased it. It was remodeled around 1953 or '54. Until then it belonged to the nuns."

Again I questioned her about the appearance of the ghost. She stuck to her story. The man was more 1903 than 1953.

"At that time there were certainly nuns here," she commented.

Had she had other uncanny experiences in this haunted apartment?

"Only this," Mrs. Kunze replied. "In my inspirational work, I found I could not work here. My guides told me this was an evil house. But I haven't heard anything."

"How long have you yourself been psychic?"

"When I was about thirteen, I was invited to a Sunday school party, and I was a stranger in the neighborhood. That was in Columbus, Ohio. About a week before the party I told my mother that I had dreamt of and had seen this party, the girls there and even the pictures on the wall — in great detail. A week later I went and recognized it all."

"Have you had any other premonitions?"

"A number of them. I do automatic writing, and

a lot of predictions have thus been dictated by me by what I call my masters, my spiritual guides."

I decided we should leave metaphysics alone, and turn to the business at hand.

"About the material obtained just now through Sybil Leek," I said, "does any of it ring a bell?

"Well, she certainly got the business with the two houses," Mrs. Kunze commented. "This house was in two locations, as you know."

"What about the trees surrounding the house?" In this part of California, trees are not common and would naturally be a landmark.

"Probably so," Mrs. Kunze said, "and she mentioned a face covered with black velvet — could that not be a nun covered with a coif?"

"Could be," I agreed. "It seems strange, though, that you haven't felt a female influence here, or have you?"

"Not at all," Mrs. Kunze confirmed, "but I felt from the looks of the *man* that he had either committed a murder or done something very wrong. I just felt it as I saw him there in the closet. I suppose he had jumped in there to avoid detection."

Evidently Mrs. Kunze had seen the ghost of the murderer while Sybil found the ghost of the victim. Now if Mrs. Kunze's prayer had indeed freed the ghost from the spot where his crime had been committed, then it was only natural that Sybil did not feel him any longer there.

At the same time, if Mrs. Kunze felt the overpowering tragedy of the murderer tied to the spot of the crime, it would have blotted out the comparatively weaker presence of the victim, who after all, was not guilty of *anything!*

I discovered that the building in its original site faced a Catholic school, and that San Bernardino has a high percentage of Catholics. Thus a convent would not have been out of place here.

On November 5, 1960, Mrs. Kunze moved out of the haunted apartment to a new house. The ghost, of course, did not move along with her, for the new apartment was free from any psychic influences; pleasant, in fact, in every sense of the word.

While she lived at the San Bernardino address, the evil atmosphere of the place seemed to have taken its toll on her. Everything she seemed to touch went wrong; her personal life was a shambles — apparently for no logical reason. The moment she moved away from the apartment, all went well. Suggestion? Not really. The facts were quite solid.

As for the empty apartment in San Bernardino, it is all ready for the new tenant to move in.

"I wouldn't take this place for anything," Sybil mumbled, as she rushed past me down the stairs and into the street.

Considering the fact that Sybil had been apartment-shopping with a vengeance at the time, the victim of the ghost in the closet must have made quite an impression on her.

At any rate, the restless nun doesn't live there anymore.

# 15
# The Ghost at the Old Merchant's House

You may remember an old movie called *The Heiress*, in which Olivia de Haviland fought against the iron will of her stern father who did not want her to marry a fortune hunter. Consequently, the heiress, as the girl was called, shut herself off from the world, having been denied the man she loved, and died a recluse in her old mansion.

The film itself was based on the well-known novel, *Washington Square*, by Henry James. James lived in the area and knew its history well indeed. The James novel is certainly based on fact, although he has embellished it with the freedom generally afforded novelists. The house, you see, didn't stand on Washington Square, New York City, but not too far away from it. It is called the Old Merchant's House, and currently is accessible to visitors as a local museum maintained privately but open to the public at certain hours.

Surrounded by old houses, some of which are in

a sad state of disrepair, the Old Merchant's House at 29 East Fourth Street, Manhattan, stands out like a jewel in a generally run-down neighborhood, not far from the infamous Bowery.

The house became the property of Seabury Tredwell, a wealthy merchant in the hardware business, as soon as it was completed by its builder. It is a Federal-style building with windows opening onto Fourth Street. Originally a lovely garden surrounded the house, but today the garden is gone. The entrance is particularly imposing, with two columns in classical style at the top of a few steps and wrought-iron lanterns adorning the door. There are three floors topped by an attic, and there is also a basement.

Inside, the furniture is still of that period. There was a banister by Duncan Phyfe, and a fine staircase leading to the upper three stories. The downstairs was filled with fine furniture (some of it also by Duncan Phyfe), a rectangular piano that is still there, and, in showcases along the walls, some of the costumes left behind.

The ghostly phenomena in the house center around Tredwell's three daughters — Phoebe, Sarah, and Gertrude. According to tradition, Mr. Tredwell did not take kindly to any suitor who seemed to want to marry his daughters for their financial status.

The main manifestations occurred in the kitchen on the ground-floor level in the rear of the house. But what used to be Gertrude's bedroom upstairs also has a presence in it from time to time. The ghost is that of a small, elegant woman dressed in the finery of the middle-nineteenth century. That this is Gertrude herself is very likely since, according to my psychic friend Ethel Johnson Meyers, it was she who died tragically here. There had been an unwanted baby, followed by disapproval of her actions by her family. How much of this can be proven objectively is doubtful, but a presence has been observed in the Old Merchant's House by several reliable witnesses, and no attempt has been made to exorcise her since, after all, this was her home.

One need not dwell upon the ghostly manifestations, as far as the curator is concerned, because she may not be aware of them. But I suggest a visit to the kitchen area, the back bedroom upstairs, and Gertrude's front bedroom. It contains a small canopied bed which, according to at least one witness, is haunted.

One eerie story told about the Old Merchant's House concerns the fireplace on the third floor. Allegedly it cannot be properly photographed. I tried my luck with a very good camera while a professional photographer who was with me at the time also photographed the fireplace. Although the fireplace did appear on both pictures, there is a strange white area around it that cannot be accounted for.

The Old Merchant's House merits a visit if only as an historical landmark and because of the well-preserved costumes and utensils of a bygone era. There is a fascinating trapdoor on one of the upper floors, connected perhaps with secret rendezvous between Gertrude and her gentleman friend outside the house. At the time, the house had a garden, and the river was not too far away. It was possible to approach the house from the East River, walk up the slanting acreage, which was then largely open, and visit the house. On the other hand, research has indicated that secret passageways existed between many of the houses in the area and the river, perhaps remnants of the Revolutionary period when escape from dangers made such precautions advisable.

Gertrude's own clothes are still preserved in the showcases and nothing in the house has been changed from its original appearance. When the house was restored by a private committee of concerned citizens, great pains were taken to present everything the way it was when the house was at its best. Architect Joseph Roberto was in charge of these sensitive restorations, and it is largely to his credit that the Old Merchant's House today truly presents a major historical attraction, as well as the tantalizing prospect of meeting up with the dainty ghost of Gertrude Tredwell herself coming down the stairs to greet the visitor!

# 16
# A Word in Parting

Remember, ghosts are people, too!

They are not monsters, aliens, evil creatures from the Great Beyond about to do you harm. Neither are they something to conjure up on a Ouija board.

If any of you should experience something out of the ordinary, and all sensible, everyday explanations just do not fit, look into the possibility of a genuine haunting. But do not jump to conclusions just because the floorboards creak or the wind howls in the chimney. It takes more than that to make a case for ghosts.

Above all, never be afraid. Approach anything of this kind with a sense of understanding and compassion, not fear. If you can help the trapped spirit we call *ghost*, speak up and offer your help. Never mind what some people may think about all this; follow your intuition.

# About the Author

Prof. Hans Holzer, Ph.D. is the author of 104 books, including *Great American Ghost Stories*, *America's Haunted Houses*, and *Ghost Hunter*. Prof. Holzer taught courses in parapsychology for eight years at the New York Institute of Technology, and lectures widely. He has been writer/producer and on-camera person or host for a number of television documentaries, such as the NBC series *In Search Of*. . . and the Metromedia special "Ghost in the House," and is currently preparing his own syndicated series. Prof. Holzer is considered a leading authority on the paranormal and unusual.

Educated at the University of Vienna, Austria, and at Columbia University, New York, Prof. Holzer received a Ph.D. from the London College of Applied Science. He lives in New York City.